To Mom -

You are amazing! You are a great mother and I can only hope to be half as good a Mom as you are. You are truly an inspiration. I love you.

A Knight With Grace

An Assassin Knights Novel
Book One

Laurel O'Donnell

ISBN: 1-940118-12-3
ISBN-13: 978-1-940118-12-3

A Knight With Grace

CHAPTER ONE

England
1183

Grace Willoughby hadn't realized her mother was so sick. Her mother lay in bed, her dark hair fanned out against the white bedding, making her face seem ghostly white. Her face was so pale. So...sickly. Rings lined her eyes. Her brow was furrowed in anguish, a sheen of perspiration dotting it. Grace wiped a strand of damp hair from her mother's brow, trying desperately to be brave. Trying desperately to be strong. But her mother was so weak. She could hear her labored breathing. She touched one of her mother's hands and it was cold. Grace wrapped her hand around her mother's in an attempt to warm her. "I love you, Mum," she whispered and tried to keep the tears from closing her throat.

Her mother grasped Grace's hand. Grace entwined her fingers through her mother's. "Be brave, my little

1

sunshine," her mother said softly.

"I will," Grace replied.

Her mother started to cough again. She was coughing a lot lately.

Blood splattered the front of Grace's dress, the dark red liquid leaving a smear on her mother's lips. Her mother quickly wiped the blood away with her sleeve. Grace knew what Mitchel, the baker's son, had told her was true. Her mother was dying. Tears rose in her eyes, blurring her vision of her mother. Grace hated the tears and quickly wiped them away with the heel of her hand so she could get a clear look at her mother. Despite her illness, her mother was still so beautiful. Her dark hair shone in the moonlight against the white cover. Grace stroked a lock of her mother's hair at her shoulder. She would miss her when she had passed. She would miss her dearly.

Suddenly, the door flung open. Her father stormed into the room, his hard cold eyes sweeping the scene. He was a short man, round in the waist and round in the face. His brow was furrowed. He pointed a trembling finger at Grace. "Get out."

"Alan!" her mother called and struggled to sit up.

Alan seized Grace by the arm and pulled her roughly from the bed.

Grace tried to get her feet beneath her, but her father yanked her toward the door, pushing her away from the bed.

Her mother shouted, her weakened voice finding a moment of strength. "Grace, don't go!"

"Father!" Grace called, alarmed at his brutal hold. He had never laid a hand on her before. Not like this.

He flung her from the room with such force she

landed on her buttocks on the cold stones of the floor. He shut the door behind her with a resounding thud. Stunned, Grace could only sit and stare, bemused and saddened, at the wooden door separating her from her mother. She looked at the guards standing on either side of the door like silent sentinels. Both men glanced away, unable to meet her gaze. She turned her gaze down at her hands splayed on the stone of the floor. Why had her father tossed her out of her mother's room? Why had he done that? What had she done?

The room behind her was silent. Strangely quiet. And then a large clatter came from inside the room followed by a roar of rage that so scared Grace she back pedaled into a shadowed corner and pulled her knees to her chest. What had happened? Was her mother dead? Was that what was making her father angry? Was he so angry because he was losing her?

Her heart twisted. She wanted to be with her mother in her last moments, to comfort her. Grace caught sight of her mother's blood on the front of her dress. Maybe her father was angry because he knew her mother only had a little time left. Yes. That must be it. Father was angry because mother was leaving him.

The handle to the door moved. The guards straightened. The door opened. Her father emerged with a strange sadness in his eyes, but his lips were clenched tight.

Grace slowly climbed to her feet. She knew she should comfort him. He was sad. But she was afraid. Afraid of his anger. What would he do if her mother was gone? Over his shoulder, she saw the flickering candle on the night table cast a dancing shadow of red onto the white blankets of her mother's bed.

He shifted his gaze to Grace. His lips curled into a sneer of disgust.

Shock raced through Grace at his hateful eyes. "Father?"

"Get away from me," he whispered savagely.

Grace took an immediate step backward, stunned. Dismayed. Hurt.

He continued past her, a small whirlwind of command and fury.

Grace quickly moved forward and looked into the room from her position outside in the hallway. Her mother lay half on the bed and half off. Her arm hung down to the floor, her fingers stained with blood. "No," Grace whispered and jerked forward to go to her. But one of the guards closed the door before her, barring her path. The image of her mother's open eyes burned into her mind. She walked stiffly to the closed door and reached for the handle.

One of the guards grabbed the handle, blocking her touch. "No, Lady Grace. She is gone."

Gone. For a moment, she didn't understand. She looked at the guard blankly. His brown eyes shone with sympathy.

Gone. Dead. Mother. Tears welled in her eyes. She was alone. She reached for the door handle again, but the guard shook his head, refusing to remove his hand and allow her entrance.

She stood for a moment, unsure. Her mother always had the answers. She always knew what to do. Now, she was gone. A swirling abyss of sadness opened inside of Grace. She turned and began to walk stiffly down the corridor. Her mother was gone. She measured each step, afraid she would miss one and tumble to the floor in a pile of useless sorrow. Mother was dead. She had to get away. Dead. She had to stop the voice in her head. It couldn't be true, but she knew it was. She ran down the corridor, racing blindly through the hallways. She didn't know where she was going, but she ran. She tripped, landing hard on her hands and knees. She stared at the stones. Dead. Tears rushed down her face, dripping onto the cold stones. She was alone. She pushed herself to her feet and dashed off again. Someone called her name, but she continued running, racing blindly away.

Grace threw herself onto the floor as sobs shook her body. Her crying echoed through the room; tremors shook her. When she was left with only ragged gasps for breaths, she looked up to find out where she was. A white clad altar towered before her; a tall wooden cross hung on the wall behind it. The chapel. She was in the chapel. She didn't remember opening the large doors and entering, but she was here. She pushed herself to her knees and clasped her hands tightly. She closed her eyes. "I don't understand why You took her. But please, Lord, please don't let me be alone. Help me find a knight to take me away from all of this. I don't want to be all alone."

CHAPTER TWO

Three months later

The rain fell to the ground in sheets of water. Grace looked up into the sky from inside the candle maker's shop. It had been three months since they put Mother into the ground. She had tried to take her mother's place and assume all of her mother's duties, but sometimes her tasks were daunting. Grace did everything she could to keep busy, but at times she simply didn't want to be alone.

"You should have gone back to the Keep when I told ya to."

Grace looked over her shoulder at the woman carefully dipping the wicks into the pot of melted wax that filled a cauldron in the middle of the shop. Minerva was a dear friend. She hunched over the cauldron, tying the wick to a stick laying across the black metal pot. Minerva's long brown hair was pulled back and tied at the base of her head. Her brown eyes focused on the pot intently, her lips pursed in concentration. Grace turned back to the empty courtyard. "You always tell me to go," she said to Minerva.

"It appears this time I was right."

Grace grimaced.

"She's right, you know," Curtis said.

Grace smiled at her friend. She enjoyed visiting with Minerva because the candle maker's shop was close to the barracks. Because of the close proximity, the shop was a perfect place for her to meet her friend, Curtis and spend time with him. Minerva didn't seem to mind. They had been meeting at the candle maker's shop since they were children, although back then it had belonged to Minerva's mother. Grace crossed her arms. "She told you to go, too."

Curtis shrugged. He was leaning back against the wall, one leg bent. His wavy, dirty blond hair fell to his strong shoulders. He wore a green tunic and black leggings. His sword was strapped to his waist. His blue eyes sparkled at Grace teasingly. "I won't ruin my dress if it gets wet."

"You don't have a dress. But you'd look stunning in one, I'm sure."

"I'd look stunning in anything I wore."

Grace rolled her eyes. "Aren't you going to be tired tonight?" She knew he had the watch later that night and should be resting.

"I wouldn't miss a chance to visit with two beautiful women!"

Minerva smiled as she dipped the wick into wax and shook her head. "Ya need to sow them wild oats, child."

"Child?" Curtis frowned. "I'm almost as old as you!"

Grace walked over to Minerva. Minerva was five years older than she, but she was already married with two children. Her children were the love of her life. Despite her young age, Minerva reminded her of her mother because of the love she held for her children. She had been a good friend of her Mother's and sometimes they would talk about her. Grace sat down at the table where Minerva was working nd tied a wick to a piece of stick.

Suddenly, a servant ducked into the room. He was dripping from the rain and his dark hair hung around his face. He scanned the room.

Grace stood up, dread snaking through her.

The servant bowed slightly. "M'lady," he greeted. "Your father is requesting your presence."

Grace glanced at Curtis as he pushed himself from the wall.

Minerva lifted her chin. "I told ya."

Grace nodded to the servant. She waved to Minerva and Curtis before following the servant through the courtyard. She picked up her skirt to dash around the puddles, but by the time she climbed the three stairs to the keep, she was drenched. Her velvet dress was streaked with water, her slippers soaked through to her feet.

The servant glanced back at her. "Would you like to change?"

Grace looked down at her dress. It was ruined, she was certain. She wiped at a streak of water across the velvet at her stomach. Her father would be angry she ruined one of her dresses. But he would also be angry she was making him wait. It didn't matter what she did, he would be angry. She shook her head and followed the servant up the stairs to her father's solar. The servant pushed the door open. The room was dark except for two candles on the table that threw small circles of light around them, and the dying fire in the hearth. The light washed over her father as he sat in a plush chair facing the fire.

Grace entered. The servant left, closing the door softly behind him.

A nervous feeling fluttered in her stomach. "Father?" she called. "You wished to see me?"

He grunted softly and pushed his rotund form to his feet. He turned toward her. A scowl of displeasure lowered his brows.

"I'm sorry about my dress, Father. I didn't want to keep you waiting."

"You look like a commoner. Where were you?" he demanded.

"I was at the candle maker's shop to purchase candles," she lied. She knew he didn't want her befriending the peasants.

His eyes narrowed in disbelief. "And she didn't offer you protection from the rain?"

"She had nothing. She offered me shelter when it started."

"I should have her whipped for not being better prepared."

Panic churned in Grace's stomach. She knew she had to distract him, draw his attention away from Minerva. "You wanted to see me."

"It is time for you to marry," he announced, a

statement of fact.

Grace had dreaded this moment. She knew it was coming, but not this close to her mother's death. She folded her hands before her, not wishing to displease him.

Her father turned his back to her and faced the fire. "You will marry Sir William de Tracy."

It took a moment to sink in. William de Tracy. Her heart heaved when she realized who he was, why the name was so familiar to her. "No!" The word was out of her mouth before she could stop it.

He whirled, fury tightening his jaw. "What did you say?"

"Father! He is a murderer. He's cursed. He's an abomination! You can't marry me to him!"

"I can and I will." His fists clenched at his sides. "Do you dare contradict my order?"

"Think of my children! Think of your grandchildren! You don't want your bloodline cursed with him as their father!"

"Do not question my judgment, girl. You will do as I say!"

She rebelled in her disbelief. Why would her father betroth her to Sir William de Tracy? The man who had killed Archbishop Thomas Becket! The knight who was damned, excommunicated by the Pope. He was sentencing her to Hell! She shook her head. "Father, you can't possibly --"

"I can and I am. You will do as you are told, girl."

"Why, Father?" she pleaded.

He stepped forward aggressively. "I don't have to explain myself to you!"

Grace bit her lip. Sir William de Tracy, her mind

kept screaming. Of all the knights, of all the men, why him? Why him? "But Father --"

Lord Alan smashed a fist against the table. "You. Will. Do. As. I. Say."

Tears entered Grace's eyes. She straightened in obedience, stifling the sob rising in her throat. She stared at him, at his furious eyes, at his hard face, at his puckered angry lips. He had never been happy with her. Not since her mother had died. He had avoided her and only issued sharp reprimands when he spoke to her at all.

She turned slowly away and walked from the room. Where was the knight she had prayed to the Lord for every night since her mother's death? Where was the man she could love? Her heart sank. That was all just a childish fantasy.

CHAPTER THREE

One Month Later

Darkness had descended over Willoughby Castle. No moon shone in the sky, no stars twinkled. It was as though the sky was hiding behind a thick coating of dark clouds.

Lord Alan Willoughby paced before the dead hearth, his fists clenched tightly. His movement as he spun to walk back over his path was quick and precise.

Servants hid out of sight near the kitchens. Even his own guards stood well over a sword's thrust away from their lord.

A guard entered the room and crossed the large expanse of the Great Hall, rushes crunching beneath his booted feet. He stopped before Lord Alan and bowed. "M'lord."

Lord Alan faced the man. "What word?"

"We've searched the entire day, m'lord. We cannot

find her."

"Cannot?!" Lord Alan roared and took a step toward his guard.

"M'lord," the guard said calmly, holding his ground. "All the men are searching. We will find her."

"But you haven't!" Lord Alan whirled away. He stood stiffly for a moment and then grabbed the edge of a wooden table. With a mighty howl of anger, he flipped the table over onto its side, sending candle sticks spinning over the rushes. Hounds scattered with whimpers. Servants ducked back behind the safety of the stone walls.

The guard took a step back, moving out of the way of the corner of the tumbling table.

"Find her!" Lord Alan commanded. "No one rests until she is back at Willoughby Castle."

"Aye, m'lord." The guard bowed slightly and departed the room.

Sir William de Tracy watched from a safe distance across the room. Not because he was afraid. Nothing scared him any more. Nothing human at any rate. He watched because he had arrived only hours before and was trying to assess what had happened. He had not been greeted upon his arrival at the castle, and no servants had attended him. He simply rode in beneath an open portcullis to an empty courtyard. A stable boy had taken his horse, but that had been the extent of his welcome. Not that he expected trumpets and fanfare as welcome, but perhaps a man to lead him into the castle. It was strange. Lord Alan had requested his presence a month ago. He had come as soon as he was able. William remembered Lord Alan as a calmer man, a man of reserve. His father and Lord Alan had been good friends, so he had seen Lord Alan many times over the years. But this man was desperate and angry.

"What are you all waiting here for?" Lord Alan screamed. "Go! Go and find her! Bring her back."

The rest of the guards near the doorway scattered out the door, leaving only William in the room with the cowering hounds and Lord Alan. William came out of the shadows as Lord Alan turned toward the hearth with a heavy sigh. "Lord Alan?"

He turned, an angry scowl on his gray brow. When he laid eyes on William, his composure turned confused for a moment as he fought for recognition. It wasn't until William was two steps away from him that identification dawned in his aged eyes. "Sir William," he said with a sigh. He shook his head. "It's good to see you, boy." He extended his hand and clasped his arm in warrior fashion.

"You requested my presence," William said.

"Yes. Yes." Lord Alan released his arm. He looked at the floor, composing his thoughts. "This is not how I anticipated speaking with you." He sat heavily in one of the chairs near the hearth. He was silent for a long moment.

William waited patiently, standing beside him. He wasn't certain what was happening, but obviously Lord Alan was very busy with something of import.

"Long ago, your father and I betrothed you and my daughter," Lord Alan said softly.

William had heard as much from his own father, but that had been long ago. He was ready to let Lord Alan out of the obligation. That was why he had come. No man would ever want his daughter married to him.

"I intend to adhere to your father's wishes."

Shock raced through William. He shook his head in confusion and denial. "You must have heard..."

Lord Alan waved his hand as if brushing away a gnat. "It makes no difference. You are still Baron of Bradninch and Lord of the Manors of Toddington, Gloucestershire, and of Moretonhampstead. Your father and I spoke for long hours about combining our lands. It was his dying wish."

William had not been there when his father passed, but he knew it had been a dream of his to grow his lands. "Lord Alan. Much has transpired since these vows were made. I certainly will not hold you or your daughter to them."

Lord Alan sighed softly. A soft cough issued from his throat, but he swallowed it down. "I am old." The coughing persisted until it grew to a hacking, overwhelming roar that all but doubled Lord Alan over. He spit on the floor and wiped his mouth with the back of his sleeve.

As Lord Alan righted himself, William noticed a thin golden chain around his neck with a pendant dangling from it. On the pendant was an engraving of a black cat.

Lord Alan tucked the pendant into his tunic. "I don't have much time left in this world. I would see my daughter well cared for."

"There must be other men."

Lord Alan straightened. "I will honor all my dues, as you should," he said. His chin rose and his eyes hardened. It looked as though he were insulted.

"Your father was a dear friend. I promised my daughter to you and you shall have her."

William didn't know what to say. It was true, everything he said. Yet, William also knew no man in their right mind would bind their daughter to him. Something else was going on here. "Very well. If it is your wish. I will wed the Lady Grace." He looked around expecting her to be standing near the kitchen door or in the shadows of the hearth. "Where is she?"

Lord Alan's hands curled into fists above the arm rests. "Whisked away. Kidnapped, I'm afraid." He struggled to his feet and lay a heavy hand on William's shoulder. "Find her. Bring her back to me."

CHAPTER FOUR

Grace held onto Sir Curtis Mortain from behind as his horse thundered down the road. Trees rushed by; the wind blew her hair back from her face and her eyes teared. The speed at which they rode was reckless and made her uneasy, but it distracted her from thinking about what she was doing. She pressed her face into Curtis's back, hiding from the wind. Her father would be furious she had fled. She scowled. She didn't care about what her father would think or do. How could he betroth her to Sir William? How could he think she would marry Sir William? He was a monster! She heard of what he had done. Entering a sacred cathedral and slaying one of God's servants. He was evil. How could her father want her to marry such a monster? Sir William was excommunicated, barred from the Church! She shook herself. She didn't want to think about it, about *him*, about her father. She would have done anything to escape the marriage. She was so glad for Sir Curtis. Surely he was the knight she had prayed for.

They rode through the darkness, the moon high overhead casting shadows onto the road before them. She wasn't afraid even though it was dark and these roads were said to be inhabited by bandits and cutthroats. She knew Curtis would protect her. As Curtis slowed the horse, she sat up and looked around. The road was empty. The sparse trees dotting the roadside gave no clue of danger.

"Fear not," Curtis said. "I'm giving my horse a rest."

She nodded. The slower pace gave her time to think. A strange sadness came over her. She was leaving the only home she had known. She was sad that it had come to this, where the only escape for her was leaving her home. Her mother would have been disappointed in her choice. But she couldn't live with her father. Not any longer. Not after the hatred she saw when she looked into his eyes. And she didn't know why. She didn't know what she had done. She tried everything to please him, even embroidering a magnificent crest on his tunic. She found all of her hard work burning in the hearth in his solar. She brought him breakfast. He left it untouched. She discovered the only way to make him happy was to avoid him, to stay out of his way.

Her thoughts shifted to the last incident that forced her departure. Betrothing her to Sir William. Why would her father do that to her? Why would he insist she marry such a man? There were other men she could marry, like Sir Curtis. Why Sir William? Her father had spoken of honor and responsibility and honoring one's vows. But there was another reason. There had to be. Could he hate her so much? She never knew what she did, but after her mother died it was different between them. He couldn't stand to be in the same room as her. He would scowl at her and his lips would twist in distaste whenever he saw her.

Still, she had been willing to stay, even though his anger and rejection hurt. She knew she had responsibilities. But this betrothal... It was too much. She would have no future. Her family would be cursed and she could not do that to children. To her children.

And then Curtis had offered to take her away. How could she say no? She would have done anything to escape the marriage. Curtis had told her such comforting stories about how they would live in his childhood cottage... She really hadn't cared. She just knew she had to leave. And he was kind to her. He was her friend.

"There," Sir Curtis said, jarring her from her thoughts. He pointed to a building in the distance. It was shadowed with glowing and dancing firelight in the windows.

"What is it?" Grace wondered.

"We will rest there."

"Do you think that wise?" she asked. Her father would have men searching every inn along the road.

"Are you saying you know better than me?" he asked with a small, condescending chuckle.

"I'm suggesting we look for something else. The guards will be searching buildings along the road."

"We will stop for food and provisions. We won't be long."

She grunted acceptingly, but it seemed like a bad idea. They should hide in the forest or keep moving.

"Did you bring coin?"

She blinked and sat back away from him. "A few coins. Like we discussed." It was all she could manage to take. She had never had need for coin, but she had a few.

He brought the horse into a cantor and steered it toward the building.

Loud, robust singing came from inside. Apprehension gripped Grace. She looked over her shoulder, half expecting her father's men to be galloping down the road to cut them off.

Curtis slid from the horse and reached up for her. She put her hands on his shoulders, but her gaze was on the wooden building. In the moonlight, the teetering inn looked barely able to stand. It seemed to sway in the small breeze. There was a stable in the back of the inn that was in no better shape. "Curtis, must we stop here? It doesn't seem like a good idea."

"Just for a moment. Do not be afraid," he proclaimed, thrusting out his chest. "I shall protect you."

Grace couldn't help but smile. He had posed in that exact same position when they were young and he pretended to fight off some invisible monster.

She nodded. Unfortunately, her father's men were not invisible monsters.

Curtis led the way into the stable. Musky and smelling of dust and hay, the stable was dark and unwelcoming. Grace stepped to the side so Curtis could stable his horse in one of the wooden stalls. When he returned to her, she took a step out of the stable, grateful for the fresh air.

"It will be best if you remain here with the horse.

Just so no one sees you."

Startled, Grace whirled on him. "What about you?"

"I shall get our food and be out straight away." He stepped past her. "No one knows me. They do not know you fled with me. It will be safer if I enter alone."

Grace glanced at the inn over his shoulder. She could see the light of a fire flickering through the shutters. She didn't want to stay in the stable, alone, and unprotected. She didn't want him to leave her.

"Don't worry," he said softly. "I would never let anything happen to you." He sauntered out of the stable.

The horse whinnied behind her as she watched Curtis enter the inn.

"Check the inn!" a voice called from outside the stable.

The voice woke Grace and she sat up straight in her position in the corner of the stall. It took her a moment to remember where she was.

She stood and hurried to the door of the stable. She craned her neck to peek out. A garrison of soldiers sat atop horses in a half moon position around the inn. She quickly backed into the stable. Her father's men! The open door of the inn cast a glow of firelight on the blue crossed pattern overlain with a black knight crest on their tunics. It was her family crest. What was she to do? Where was Curtis? He had been in the inn for a long time. She must have dozed off, she realized. Dread filled her and she looked around the stable.

Curtis's horse and one other were in the stalls, but there was no sign of Curtis. He hadn't come back. She would have to hide. She refused to go back to her father, to the castle. Two empty stalls completed the stable. She moved to the last stall. The stall was filled with hay.

"Look in the stable!"

Apprehension filled Grace, twisting her stomach. There was no other choice. She raced toward the corner of the stall and dug into the hay quickly. She dove into the hole she made and pulled hay down over her head and around her body so it covered her. She hoped she was covered well enough to block her body from the view of the men. She tucked her feet in, pulled her knees against her chest and tucked her skirt around her feet. She reached out and pulled more hay around her and leaned back, hoping to stay invisible to their probing gazes. They couldn't find her! Her heart hammered in her chest. Her breath came in short gasps. She couldn't see because of the hay and she closed her eyes to pray.

CHAPTER FIVE

Grace heard footsteps crunching on the brittle hay. They stopped for a moment and then started again, coming toward her. She held her breath and didn't move. Not an inch. She clenched her hands in the velvet fabric of her skirt and squeezed her eyes closed tightly. She couldn't go back. She wouldn't. Never again.

A long moment past and she thought at any moment she would be seized and hauled from her hiding place. She waited. Her heart pounded in her chest and in her ears. Still, she waited. But no one laid hands on her and eventually the sounds of the steps moved out of the stable, fading into the distance. She let a soft sigh issue from her lips. She was still too afraid to leave her hiding spot. She was still too fearful she would be discovered. So she remained hidden. Alone. Where was Curtis?

Her hand itched as the hay scratched it, but she dared not move.

More footsteps broke the silence.

They've come back! They knew she was hiding in the stable and they returned for her! Grace held her breath. Tears entered her eyes.

The footsteps seemed hurried as they rushed into the stable. They moved back and forth along the aisle before the stalls. "Grace?"

She thought she recognized the voice, but then she realized it might be wishful thinking, so she remained hidden beneath the hay.

"Grace!"

She did recognize the voice! She shoved the hay from her head. "Curtis!" she gasped.

He rushed back to the stall she was in and stood in the opening as she pushed the hay away from her body. She stood up and dusted the hay from her dress. "Are they gone?"

A crooked smile settled on his lips. "You look like a wench after a tumble."

She stepped out of the stall, gently pushing him back. "Are they gone?" She rushed to the doorway and peered out.

"They've gone."

Grace whirled on him, angry and fearful. "Where were you? We should have left hours ago!"

"I'm sorry. You were right. We should not have stopped here," Curtis agreed. He held up a small bag. "But I got bread for us."

What had taken him so long? All that time for a bag of bread? She eyed it doubtfully, but nodded. "We should go before they come back."

Curtis pulled his horse from the stall and helped her to mount. He swung up behind her, his arms going around her as he grabbed the reins.

Grace dusted more hay from her hair as they rode out of the stable. She noticed a dark-haired woman standing in the doorway of the inn, swaying her hips back and forth, smiling at Curtis as they past. When Grace twisted around in the saddle to look at Curtis, she saw he wore the same smile the woman had. He nodded to the woman before spurring the horse down the road.

They stopped at the side of a small stream to rest. The sun was directly overhead, beating down through the foliage of the forest trees to dapple the leaf-covered ground.

Grace moved to the stream and bent, rinsing off her face with the cool, fresh water. They had been traveling all morning and she was hot, sore, and hungry. She sat back on her bottom. She should have felt relief and joy, but she only felt sad and lonely. She cast a glance over her shoulder.

Curtis brushed his dark hair from his eyes. He was tall and strong, a fine knight. But he had no idea how to care for her or for himself. He was too used to being sheltered inside a castle, too impulsive and self-serving. She put her hands against her forehead. What was she doing? This suddenly seemed like a very bad idea. It was too late to go back. Besides, she never would. She would run and live the life of a commoner before marrying Sir William. Yes, she was doing the right thing. The only thing she could do. Grace stood as Curtis tied the brown horse to a nearby branch. He reached into one of the bags tied to the saddle. He pulled out a small loaf of bread and took a large bite.

Grace walked over to him. "Might I have some bread?"

He opened the bag and looked inside. Then he glanced at the small piece of bread remaining in his hand. He held it out to her.

She stood for a moment, shocked. "Is that all that is left?"

"I'm afraid so."

"You ate the rest of it?" she asked, taking the bread from his hand.

"I need to keep my strength to defend you!" he protested.

Irritation grated on her. He had eaten the bread they needed to hold them over until the next town! And she had eaten none of it. Good Lord! How selfish Curtis was! He was like a child, a boy who never thought of others. She took the offered bread and broke it in half. She gave him some. He was right. He needed his strength. She stared down at the bread in her hand. She should have been starving. Perhaps it was nervousness, perhaps it was the uncertainty of the future, but she wasn't hungry.

He handed her a flask.

She took a sip of the warm ale and handed it back to him.

"You look pale. Are you feeling all right?" Curtis asked.

Grace looked at him in disbelief. "I'm worried. I'm frightened. I'm tired."

"Do you want to go back?"

"Never!" she hissed. She shook her head and

waved away her worry. "It's too late. I can't go back. And I don't want to." She looked at him, suspiciously. "Do you?"

"I am yours to serve," he said with a slight bow.

"Stop it," she admonished. "Don't make fun of me. I want to know if you are having doubts. I need to know if you want to return to Willoughby Castle."

He took her hands into his and looked sincerely into her eyes. "I won't leave you, Grace. You don't have to worry. I will only return if you want to return."

Grace sighed softly. "Thank you."

Curtis nodded and tugged her toward a tree. "Sit here. Rest." He sat on the ground and leaned back against a tree. "Come rest your head on my shoulder. I will tell you of our future."

Yes, a distraction. It was exactly what Grace needed. She sat beside him, tucking her skirt about her thighs and ankles. He opened his arms and she leaned her head against his chest.

"We shall live in the woods far from Willoughby Castle. In the fall, the leaves shall turn to a brilliant red and gold." He picked up a strand of her hair. "Much the color of your locks."

Grace closed her eyes, imagining the picture his words painted. Beautiful. Peaceful. Serene. She needed that kind of calm in her life. She desperately wanted to block everything else out.

"My father hath bequeathed a small cottage to me upon his dying bed. It is slightly north and west of Sir Breton's lands, on the border. I grew up there. I'm sure it will need some work, as no one has lived there for years. But it will be perfect for us. It won't be what you are used to. It is no castle."

Grace didn't care how small it was. She didn't care where it was. She only cared it was not with her father. "Is there room for a garden?"

"We will plant a garden with enough food to sustain us. I shall chop wood for the fire."

"We will have a goat. And some ducks," Grace added. She would be with her friend. It would be a happy place.

"And my horse and sword."

Grace nodded. "Of course." His horse. She sighed softly. Their images of their future lives were vastly different. She still thought he imagined being a knight in a cottage. He wasn't really thinking about a home or a garden. He was not the knight she had prayed for. She had thought he might be; she had convinced herself he could be, but she knew deep in her heart, he was not her knight. Still, he was the next best thing. And he was her friend.

"I'm sorry, Sir William, but I have not seen a woman matching that description come this way."

William handed the inn keeper two shillings. "Thank you." He walked toward the door. This was the only inn on the road. He didn't think she would have come this way, too many people would have seen her. He also spoke to Captain Trenton as he rode back to the castle. The Captain assured him she had not come this way. He said they had already searched the inn. William searched anyway. Things could be overlooked and he had this feeling...

He paused at the door of the inn to glance around the room. It was almost empty, only two tables with patrons eating at them. Two men, travelers by the looks of them. It made no sense. She couldn't have just disappeared. Had her kidnapper taken her the opposite way? Into the forest? Could his instincts be wrong? He opened the door and stepped out into the sunny day.

He glanced around the yard. His gaze fell on the stable. A dark-haired woman emerged carrying a bucket in two hands.

He moved to her and took the bucket from her. It was full of water. "Are you taking this to the inn?"

"Aye," she said, cautiously looking him over.

He carried the bucket to the door of the inn. She hurried to step in front of him, standing rather close to him. "Aren't you a helpful one? And so strong. Surely there is some way I can repay you." Her smile was coy and seductive.

William stared down at her. Her teeth were brown and a front one had fallen out. He was not aroused by her in the slightest. "There is one way." He set the bucket down.

"Oh," she laughed low in her throat.

"Have you seen a noble woman with golden hair?"

She placed her hands on his chest and then laced them about his neck, pressing her body against his. "I see lots of noble women."

"The one I'm looking for is fairly young. Maybe eighteen summers. It would have been early today or yesterday." She sighed and her breath fanned his face. It was all he could do to not pull away from the odor of dead fish.

She stepped back and put her hands on her hips, jutting out her breasts. "Yea, I saw 'er." She looked him over slowly. "But she couldn't satisfy the knight she was with like I could."

"A knight?" William repeated. "Do you know who he was?"

"I think he said his name was Curtis. Sir Curtis. Yes. He was a large man, but you are so much bigger." She smiled through her gap-toothed mouth.

A knight had kidnapped Lady Grace. Sir Curtis. William looked down the road. "Which way did they go?"

"They rode off in that direction." She pointed away from the castle. "Down that road."

William picked out two shillings from his pouch and handed them to the girl. "For your time." He turned away from the woman toward the stable and his mount.

"I have more time!" she called after him.

William didn't turn back.

"Knights," she whispered with contempt and picked up the bucket, carrying it inside the inn.

CHAPTER SIX

"How much farther?" Grace asked, wearily. They had been on the road for over a week and she had begun to think Curtis had no cottage and they would wander the roads forever. Her bottom was numb, her limbs tired. Her entire body ached.

"Not much farther," Curtis replied.

He wasn't very convincing. There had been many times during the week they had veered off the road and hid in the woods to avoid her father's men. And every time she saw them, she was reminded of her father, of the hate she saw in his eyes. The days were long and she had too much time to think. Too much time to think about why her father would have scorned her in such a way. At first, she thought it was his sadness and anger at losing her mother. She felt the same anguish, the same loneliness. But every time she approached her father, he would scowl at her and his lips would thin, as if he was angry with her. It must have been something she had done. As she thought back to the days, before her mother's death and after, there was nothing she could think of. Nothing she had done to cause such animosity in her father.

Curtis pointed down the road ahead of them. "See the bend in the road? We turn off there and head west. We're almost there."

Excitement soared within her. The fatigue and aches in her body disappeared and she was energized by anticipation. Finally! The horse suddenly seemed to be moving very slowly. The animal was just walking. Curtis wasn't urging him into a cantor. How could he be so patient? She wanted to leap from the horse and race ahead. She shifted her position.

Curtis chuckled. "Patience, little dove. We'll have the rest of our lives to live there."

His voice sounded indifferent. Bitter, almost. She swiveled to look at him. "Aren't you happy?"

"Of course I am," he said and smiled at her.

The smile didn't reach his eyes. She couldn't help but notice his lack of enthusiasm. He seemed somehow distant. She couldn't figure out what it was. She lay a hand on his arm. "I am truly thankful for you, Curtis."

"I know," he said softly.

She turned away from him to look at the bend in the road which grew closer and closer. She bowed her head. Maybe he had reason for reserve. "Curtis, have you thought about what would happen if my father's men come looking for me here?"

"Of course! You will hide. I will tell them that I am here alone, tending my lands."

She looked back at him, his warm eyes, his gentle and encouraging grin. He seemed to have thought this through. Perhaps she was wrong. Perhaps he was just as tired as she. Her gaze swept his face. It was clean shaven and rugged, confident. "I would never implicate you. If we are discovered, I would say I forced you to take me."

Curtis laughed. "And who would believe you?"

Grace was quiet for a moment. A question nagged at her and she had to ask it aloud. "Why are you helping me, Curtis?"

"I am your friend."

It was the way he said it. As if he had said it a thousand times before. Just words. There was no feeling behind the words. She turned to look back at the road. It didn't matter. She had escaped with Curtis and this would be her life now. "If you want to leave me here, I will understand."

"Leave you? Then who would protect you?"

She looked back at him again and pressed a kiss to his cheek.

His brows rose in surprise.

"I can't tell you what this means to me."

Curtis looked away to the side and the dirt of the road.

"You've freed me," Grace whispered.

"Don't be too certain. You'll have to look over your shoulder all of the time. Pretend to be someone else. That's not freedom, if you ask me."

Grace scowled at him. It certainly was better than the life her father had wanted for her with Sir William.

Curtis guided the horse forward, turning off the main road, moving to the right.

Grace didn't see a path through the high stalks of

grass.

"I've taken this way many times when I was a boy," Curtis said fondly. "The cottage is just ahead. Over that ridge."

Grace sat straight in the saddle, straining to see the building. She knew it wouldn't be grand, but she imagined a sturdy structure with a small side garden. "You grew up here as a boy?"

"Yes. My father and I. I used to play with my brother in these very fields."

"You have a brother? You never mentioned him."

"He left when I was five to find his way in the world. He sells his sword."

"A mercenary? Has he ever worked for my father?"

"No. I haven't seen him in years."

A brother. Strange, he had never mentioned him. But she had never asked. She looked ahead, searching for the cottage. "What type of games did you play with your brother?"

He shrugged. "King and peasant, sometimes. Mostly knights. We would use sticks as swords." He pointed ahead. "There. There it is."

Grace saw the thatched roof first. As they rode closer, she saw the rest of the building. It was a small, simple square structure. There was no door to the entrance leaving a gaping hole and darkness inside. The entire area was overgrown with weeds. It was clear no one had lived here for a very long time. It wasn't quite what she had imagined. Perhaps the inside was in better shape. Trepidation spread through her. And then, she lifted her chin. It didn't matter. This was her home. With Curtis. What had she expected? It will be fine, she told herself. We will make it work.

He reined his horse in before the open door and dismounted. He looked around, gazing from here to there, as if lost in memory. Then, he turned to Grace and helped her from the horse.

Grace glanced at the overgrown doorway, the weeds twisting and turning as if to block her way. There was a rectangular area beside the cottage that seemed particularly overgrown with thick weeds and tall stalks of grass. It must have been the garden at one time, but it was almost non-existent now. If it weren't for the lone vine of cucumbers she might not have recognized it.

She suddenly felt Curtis's gaze on her. She hadn't realized she was wringing her hands until he grasped one. "Would you like to go home now?"

Shocked, she pulled her hand free of his. "This is my home now. This is *our* home. It just needs a little...work." A little work? They would have to pull all the weeds and replant. She didn't know if they would even get any food this year. As she gazed at him, a slow realization dawned in her. "You thought I would return home?"

Curtis bowed his head, ignoring the question. He gently pulled her toward the doorway. "Come. See the inside." But he stopped as a figure appeared in the doorway and stepped out into the daylight. "Who are you and what are you doing here?"

The man was dressed in chainmail with a sword strapped to his side. He wore no helm, his dark hair falling to his shoulders in waves. He glanced at Grace. Blue eyes burned into her, sweeping her from head to toe. She was surprised she wasn't afraid of this man.

"I'm here to take Lady Grace home," the knight proclaimed in a calm, assured voice.

"Who are you?" Grace asked.

"Sir William de Tracy."

CHAPTER SEVEN

Sir William sized up Sir Curtis with a quick glance. He was a tall man, but not of impressive stature. He was young. Maybe just a few years older than Lady Grace, if even that.

Curtis's lip curled in a sneer and he stepped back, drawing his sword. "You shant be taking her anywhere."

William had known it would come to this. He held up his hands. "I don't want to fight you."

"Of course not," Curtis snarled. "You've done enough murdering for a lifetime. You will have to fight if you intend to take Lady Grace, for I have no intention of giving her up."

With a reluctant sigh, William pulled his sword from its sheath. "So be it." William was skilled in sword fighting and he was sure he would defeat this young knight standing so brazenly defiant before him. He hoped that perhaps he could teach the brash young hot head a lesson without hurting him.

Curtis swung first, two quick blows.

William easily deflected them, but he was too close to the cottage and had nowhere to retreat, so he eased to the side. Curtis attacked that side with another swipe, intent on keeping William cornered. William parried the blows, the tings of the blades ringing out through the air. William quickly moved the other way, away from the cottage.

They circled, each man holding his sword up, and each sharp, deadly tip pointed at its opponent.

"Murderer," Curtis hissed.

William betrayed no emotion. He had grown used to the accusation and the derogatory names and comments others threw at him. He had lived with them for a long time.

"You don't deny it."

"It would not matter what I said. You've cast your judgment," William stated. He watched the young knight's style, looking for a way to disarm him. Curtis made many mistakes. He kept his sword too low. His grip was too loose. His eyes focused on his opponent's blade. It was a wonder he was still alive. But William knew Curtis had not been trained as he had. The young knight had been in no wars, only mock battles, and play. It was an entirely different affair if your life depended on your sword skill. He glanced at Lady Grace and was pleased to see she seemed to be unharmed and had the sense to back away from the battle.

"Imagine the hero I would become if I slay you," Curtis said with a cold glint in his eye and scorn twisting his lips. He lunged forward, but quickly changed his move to arc a blow at William's head.

William could have easily lunged in and stabbed

Curtis in the chest. Instead, he stepped aside and the tip of Curtis's sword hit the ground, a small cloud of dirt spraying up upon impact. William kicked Curtis's hand and the sword went flying through the air.

Stunned, Curtis stared.

William worked out his wrist, moving his sword around in a circle. He moved to the side, giving Curtis safe passage to his weapon. "Pick it up."

Curtis quickly dashed to the spot his weapon had fallen and grabbed it. He scoffed. "Luck."

William knew luck had nothing to do with it. If Curtis was a smarter opponent, he would have known that and run away. But, as William mentally predicted, he didn't.

Curtis approached, cautiously now, not as cocky.

William bent his knees slightly, preparing for the attack. He was no longer in the mood to teach this young knight. He wanted this done quickly so he could return Lady Grace to her father. He didn't want to kill the knight, just incapacitate him enough to allow them to leave unhindered. Perhaps a cut on his leg.

Curtis took a quick moment, assessing William before he attacked, swinging from the left and then the right, moving forward with quick vicious strikes.

William blocked both blows and struck back with brutal force, pushing Curtis into the grassy field. He continued his attack, hitting Curtis's sword again and again, leaving him on the defensive. He swung left, left, left and then a quick right. The change-up was difficult for his opponent to block. Curtis just managed to switch his sword in time to deflect it.

And then William attacked the right. After only one swing, he kicked Curtis back. The young knight staggered, but kept his footing to counter a thrust to his body. He used only one hand and William saw his moment. He caught Curtis's sword with his blade and spun his wrist. Because of Curtis's loose grip, the sword spun through the air and landed in the long grass.

William put the tip of his sword to Curtis's throat. "Yield," he ordered.

For a moment, Curtis couldn't move. He stared in disbelief. Shocked, he slowly lifted his hands.

William waited. He gently pressed the tip of his sword against Curtis's throat to remind him of his choice.

"I yield," Curtis said through gritted teeth.

"Then be on your way." William lowered his sword and turned to Lady Grace. He sheathed his weapon. He expected to see a glimmer of happiness in her face, or even for her to run to him and throw her arms around him in gratitude. He expected to be the hero for once in his life. But her eyes were wide and her lower lip pouted. "You need not fear, Lady Grace. You are free now."

Tears welled in her large eyes. Were those tears of happiness? He scowled. Something was not right here. He heard a shifting of clothing behind him.

Grace lifted a hand and stepped forward. "Curtis, no!"

William turned in time to see Curtis coming toward him, a dagger raised high. Instinctively, William thrust his arm out behind him to catch Grace and sweep her aside as Curtis brought the dagger down. William turned away and the dagger hooked into a link in his chain mail. Curtis pulled the dagger free and lifted it for another blow. William caught his wrist. They struggled, both pulling and pushing to get the other into a weak position. William hooked a foot behind Curtis's leg and shoved him aside with all his strength.

Curtis fell heavily, dropping his hands to catch himself.

William stood over him, his legs bent, his arms out defensively, awaiting Curtis's rise. Curtis remained on his hands and knees, his head bent and his long blonde hair concealing his face. William cautiously stepped around to the front of Curtis, ready for him to lash out or jump to his feet. Was this some sort of trick to draw him closer? Then one drop of blood fell onto the dirt ground near Curtis's hand, then another.

Curtis lifted his gaze to William. He sputtered and blood splashed from his mouth.

William scanned him, glancing quickly over Curtis's body. And then he saw what had happened. The dagger Curtis held had been twisted up in his fall and impaled him. William straightened. He had been in enough battles to know this kind of wound was fatal. The fight was over. And still, despite his less than honorable attack from behind, William felt a twinge of regret. It didn't have to end this way. He could have run.

"Curtis?" Grace called.

Curtis held out a shaking hand to her.

William blocked her path as she came forward. "There is nothing to be done."

Grace surged around him and dropped to her

knees at Curtis's side. She took Curtis's face into her hands, brushing his hair from his forehead.

William's mouth dropped open in surprise. That tender touch made everything clear. William knew in that instant. She had not been kidnapped. She was fleeing. He snapped his mouth closed. Of course she was, he thought. As she should be. He gritted his jaw, his thoughts bitter. He wasn't certain if he was angry with her or her father. It didn't matter.

Curtis turned over, revealing the dagger lodged in his chest. He lay his head in her lap, staring at the sky above.

Grace's tears fell onto the young knight's face, trailing paths of despair. She continued to stroke his forehead and cheeks, wiping the blood from his mouth with her sleeve.

William turned away. Let the two spend his last moments together in privacy. Of course, he did not like to see his future wife grieving over another man, but there was naught to do about it now. Future wife, he thought in mockery as he stepped into the cottage. He patted the neck of his horse. He had kept the black war horse inside so they wouldn't know he was here. This was not quite what he had expected. Lord Alan told him she had been kidnapped. Everyone was looking for her. Didn't he know? She had run away! William couldn't blame her. What woman would want to marry him? But for a moment, William had believed what he was doing was worthwhile and just. He bowed his head, leaning it against Hellfire's neck. How wrong he had been!

CHAPTER EIGHT

Grace gently stroked Curtis's cheek even after he had long since slipped away. This was her fault. He would still be alive if he hadn't agreed to take her away. Tearfully, she pressed her forehead to his. He would still be alive if he hadn't have been her friend. Why? Why would the Lord take him away? Why would the Lord do this to her? After all her praying for her knight to come and save her, this is what He brought to her instead. She had prayed every day, every spare moment. What else did He want? She sat up and swiped at her eyes with her sleeve, only to freeze. Blood stained the hem of the sleeve. A new wave of anguish crested over her, and with it came resolve and anger. She had prayed enough. She had to be strong and depend on herself. If God wasn't answering her prayers, then she would save herself.

She eased Curtis's head to the ground, silently thanking him. She backed away to a nearby tree, pressing her back against it as she sat. She lifted her knees, encircling them with her arms. She was not going home. She would fight. She would do what she had to. She was not returning to Willoughby Castle. Because if she did, everything Curtis had done for her would be for naught. Curtis. She bowed her head to her knees and grief washed over her, letting out a torrent of sorrow. Tears rolled down her cheeks. Dead. Curtis was dead. Just like her mother. Death was following her everywhere.

That accursed Sir William! He had done this! He had taken him away. Why did he have to come after her?

"M'lady..."

She lifted her head to find Sir William standing before her. Vile murderer! She should have expected nothing less of this monster. He had slain the archbishop, so what did the life of a simple knight mean to him? Now he had murdered her friend, too. "You killed him," she whispered, her voice ragged.

Sir William stood stoically before her. No emotion crossed his rugged face. Icy blue eyes gazed at her. Finally, he turned and moved into the cottage. When he emerged, he was holding a shovel.

Grace was surprised when he began to dig a grave, surprised at this honorable act. She lifted her chin. That still didn't change the fact he had murdered Curtis nor that his soul was damned for all eternity.

The sun was setting, spreading a deep red across the sky, when William finally finished burying Curtis. He patted the shovel on top of the grave.

Grace stood in the shade of the tree, watching William bury Curtis. With Curtis gone, Sir William would take her back to her father and insist she marry him. But she never would. Her life was being buried with Curtis in that grave. Their life. She would not betray him. She would never make his death, his sacrifice, meaningless. She would never marry William. But how was she going to stop it now? Desperation filled her. She couldn't just stand here and do nothing! She glanced over her shoulder into the woods. The leaves swayed in a soft breeze as if beckoning her. She could run. But she knew that would be even worse. Without protection, she wouldn't stand a chance against the outlaws and bandits roaming the woods. And Sir William would come after her anyway. She was trapped. She crossed her arms tightly over her chest. She was not going back to her father.

William straightened, wiping a hand across his sweat drenched forehead. He arched his back. He had removed his chainmail armor and his gambeson and worked in a tunic.

She lifted her chin slightly and determination filled her. She prepared for a fight.

He put the shovel on his shoulder and turned to her.

Her entire body clenched in dread. He would take her back to her father, regardless of whether she wanted to go or not. The thought was agony. The thought was horrible. She wouldn't do it. She wouldn't return. She couldn't. She squeezed her arms.

He bowed his head and his long dark, damp strands fell forward. "We'll stay here for the night and start out in the morning."

She didn't acknowledge she heard him. She looked at Curtis's grave, a lump rising in her throat. Grateful relief swept through her. She had one more night to think of a solution. She would do anything not to return to her father.

He lowered his chin to his chest. "I'm sorry for your loss."

Shocked at the sincerity in his voice, she looked at him. Dark strands hid his face from her.

"You can stay inside the cottage. I will remain outside."

For a moment, she couldn't move. It was more sympathy than her father had shown her after her mother's death. He was allowing her grieving time. She had to use the time wisely. Yes, she would miss Curtis and she did grieve for him. But she had to think of her future. There would be time to mourn him later. She glanced again at Curtis's grave before brushing by William to enter the cottage and begin planning.

William sat beneath a nearby tree with his horse, Hellfire, standing nearby. The moon was far overhead, casting the surroundings in a surreal muted glow. Curtis's steed whinnied softly, perhaps missing his owner. William had tied him to another tree where there was plenty of grass to feed on. He lifted his head to gaze at the moon. It had been almost fifteen years since he had last gotten a good night's sleep. He had spent time fighting in Jerusalem, had participated in many skirmishes, had nearly lost his own life many times in the frenzied madness of battle, but that was not what kept him up at night. It was the blood. Every time he closed his eyes, he saw pools of innocent blood filling his mind's eye. In his dark dreams, he often found himself staring down at his hands, seeing them covered in dark red liquid. He wondered if his friends had this much trouble sleeping.

He doubted Reginald FitzUrse had any trouble sleeping. Reginald was always confident in his actions, never regretting them. It was for the king, Reginald would say. Everything they had done had been for the king. Reginald's loyalty was to King Henry, even above God. His excommunication never seemed to bother him. Reginald was tough, always fighting for what he believed in with the courage of a lion, but he was also angry and headstrong. After all this time, William wondered if it hadn't been for Reginald's anger, if they would have sought to bring the archbishop before the king. William thought back to that fateful night. A colder night. A December night.

Two monks clad in brown robes opened the doors of the cloister for the four knights. The four knights, William, Reginald, Richard le Brey and Hugh de Morville, entered the monastery, each man's face filled with grim determination. Reginald led the way into the hall. William nodded at one of the monks he past. He couldn't help but notice the fear and anxiety in the young monk's dark eyes.

Long tables lined the hall and monks ate quietly at them.

"Where is Thomas Becket?" Reginald demanded.

The monks looked up at him. Some set aside their food and drink, but none said a word.

Richard Le Brey stepped forward. "Where is the traitor?"

"We bear a message from King Henry!" Reginald added. "Speak up!"

William glanced at Reginald in surprise. They had no message from the king. Perhaps he meant they were here on the king's mission. Still, the half truth made him uneasy.

Finally, a man dressed in white robes rose from one of the tables. His bearing, his demeanor was different than the others. He clearly commanded respect. "I am here, FitzUrse," Archbishop Thomas Becket said. "Why do you disturb these monks at mealtime?"

"By the king's orders, you are to return with us to England," Reginald commanded.

"I do not answer to the king, but to One in higher authority. I will not return to England."

William gaped at this, as did the rest of the knights. Defying King Henry's order was unthinkable. "You defy the king?" William asked, shocked.

The archbishop looked at William and his gaze softened. "I answer only to one rule. His rule."

His rule. The Lord's rule. Uncertainty immediately filled William. Is that what he was doing by being here? Is that what this mission meant? Was he placing king over God? Before he could answer, or question himself further, Reginald stepped forward.

"All who are on the side of the king, hinder the archbishop!" Reginald ordered the monks. "Do not let him leave!" He whirled and stormed from the hall.

William stood still for a second longer, as his comrades moved out of the hall, following FitzUrse. Would they return to England empty handed? Would they return as failures? His gaze moved over the hall. Many of the monks mumbled amongst themselves. Some rose and gathered together near the archbishop. William began to turn, but locked eyes with the archbishop.

"Turn from this path, knight," the archbishop commanded.

William knew there would be no turning back from this. The monks knew they came for the archbishop. Others would know of their mission after they left. They would be seen as failures if the archbishop did not return with them. They would be laughed at. Ridiculed. He turned and followed his friends from the hall.

William had missed that first opportunity to abort their mission, to talk his friends into leaving. But he knew Reginald would never have left regardless of any arguments William might have presented to him. Reginald would never have run from the mission. Thomas Becket had been doomed from the moment the king uttered the words 'What a parcel of fools have I nourished in my house, that not one of them will avenge me of this upstart clerk!'.

With a sigh, William knelt in the dirt, as he did every night, and said a prayer for the archbishop's soul.

Sleep came sporadically for Grace. She sat in a corner, as far away from the door as possible. The mattress had bugs and moldy straw in it. Her stomach grumbled. The uncertainty of her future haunted her. How was she going to get out of this? Her thoughts shifted to William. What of that murderer? He was cursed for what he had done, doomed to hell, excommunicated. Why would her father have betrothed her to him, knowing his grandchildren would be cursed as the spawn of evil? She didn't understand her father. Not his sudden hatred of her, nor his decisions. Had her mother's death driven him to insanity? She lowered her chin to her chest and closed her eyes. He would be furious that she ran away, that she had defied his order. He had commanded her to marry William and she had defied him. He wouldn't tolerate it. Maybe Curtis was lucky to be dead.

She slept little that night, fitfully tossing and turning. Having come up with no plan for her future, despite her praying, she remained in the cottage when morning came. She paced, desperately trying to come up with a plan of escape.

The sun was high overhead when William called to her, "Lady Grace. Are you hungry?"

She rubbed her stomach. Yes. She was hungry! She and Curtis had eaten very little on their trip. She hesitantly moved to the open doorway, her hunger overriding her caution. She had to keep her strength up for the coming ordeal.

Sir William stood over a small fire, roasting something on a spit.

Grace lifted her chin, debating whether to refuse him. But the smell of the meat made her mouth water and she left the safety of the cottage to approach the campfire.

He didn't look at her as she approached. He bent to turn the spit.

She sat across the fire from him where she could observe him while pretending to look at the food. His dark hair hung in waves to his shoulders. He knelt on one knee, the other bent before him. He wore a simple green tunic and black leggings. His sword was strapped to his waist.

He reached across to her, holding out a small loaf of bread.

She took it with a mumbled, "Thank ye." She told herself to go slow as she bit into it. She didn't know when she would eat next. The bread was fresh and flavor erupted in her mouth. Her eyes almost rolled in enjoyment. She finished the loaf in only a moment. It was delicious!

"I thought he kidnapped you, but I see I was wrong."

Grace lifted her gaze to him. "Why would you think Curtis kidnapped me?"

"Your father told me."

Her father thought she was kidnapped? Maybe he would be relieved she was safe. Maybe... But she didn't think so.

"When you disappeared, your father was concerned. You are lady of Willoughby Castle. You would make for a fine ransom."

Ransom? That had never been their plan. She and Curtis were going to build a future together. She shook her head and looked back at the spit and the meat William was roasting. It looked like rabbit. "I paid Curtis to take me away."

William snapped his gaze to her in surprise, raking her from head to toe thoughtfully. "You must have been very desperate to get out of the marriage."

It wasn't just the marriage. She wanted to be away from her father. "We were going to make a home here."

His gaze shifted to look at the cottage before

turning back to her. "It didn't occur to you that this would be the very first place your father would look?"

She opened her mouth and then closed it. It hadn't.

"It must not have occurred to Sir Curtis, either. Although any soldier would know that."

"What are you saying?" Grace demanded.

William shook his head. "Just that if I were taking the woman I loved away..."

She straightened and corrected him by declaring, "He was my friend."

"Pardons. If I were taking my friend away, I would go to a place that had no connection to me. If someone was trying to find you, home would be the first place to look. Next, any relations. Aunts, cousins. Seems suspicious to me, that's all. Why would he bring you to the first place he knew they would look?"

Grace scowled. She stared down at her slippered feet. "Perhaps he didn't know they were going to search here. His father died a long time ago. He said he left this cottage to him."

"He grew up here."

Grace nodded. "Yes. But he had not been here for some time." She scowled and raised her gaze to him. "You shouldn't belittle a dead man. It is dishonorable."

"I am not belittling him. I am simply pointing out facts. Once I found out his name, Sir Curtis Mortain, he was easy to find. *You* were easy to find."

Easy to find, her mind repeated. Curtis would never have wanted her to be found! This was to be their home. They had talked about the garden and...

Why would he bring her to his family home? Doubt plagued her and this made her angry. "Your logic doesn't make sense. Curtis had nowhere else to go. This was a good choice. I mean... why would Curtis have wanted my father to find me? He would have been thrown in the dungeon!"

William's gaze shifted to the rabbit. He cut off a piece of meat with his dagger and handed it to her. "You said you paid him. How much?"

She stared at the rabbit he offered, her anger outweighing her hunger. Curtis would never have brought her here if he knew her father would find them! Would he? "It doesn't matter."

William lowered the rabbit. "But it does. He was a young knight. If you had paid him enough, he wouldn't need you. Maybe he only wanted the coin."

His words made her re-think her recent time with Curtis. Every time they had stopped, Curtis had left her. Almost as if he were anxious to be away from her. What had he been doing? She swallowed down the uncertainty, but it had already snaked a path into her mind. Sadness filled her. Had he really deceived her? "He said we would live here."

William's gaze moved slowly over her. "You should consider yourself lucky, Lady Grace. He could have simply killed you."

Shock rocked her. "Curtis was honorable," she defended vehemently. "He would never have hurt me! We were friends!" It couldn't be! William was just trying to confuse her. She had thought that perchance Curtis might come to love her someday. But more nagging thoughts came to her, more questions. Curtis had never kissed her. He had not even tried! Stunned at the realization, she turned and slowly made her way back into the cottage.

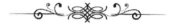

William combed down Hellfire, speaking to him in soft tones. His horse had been his only one true friend through all of this. And they were both getting older. The horse tossed his head and William patted him on the nose. "She just needs time." He cast a glance at the opening to the cottage. Lady Grace had not emerged since earlier that morn, although he had heard her moving about. She must be thirsty, if not hungry. He was glad she ate a loaf of bread. Perhaps he had been too harsh, too early. After all, the man she had paid to take her away just died. Died. William shook his head as he moved to put the brush back into his saddle bag. Curtis had been brash and reckless attacking a trained knight. But William had not wanted him to die. After the brutal fighting in Jerusalem, he had made a vow never to kill again. And he hadn't. Sir Curtis had fallen on his own dagger after a less than honorable attack.

Grace's accusation that he had killed Curtis pierced him like a dagger. While he knew he had not killed the young knight, the fact she believed he did was enough to tighten his chest in despair. He had wanted to shout at her that it was not true; he had wanted to shake her into seeing he had not hurt Curtis, that it had been Curtis's own foolish, dishonorable actions. But in his experience, people believed what they wanted to believe no matter what one did or said.

He looked down the overgrown road and

wondered how long it would be before her father's men came for Lady Grace.

Footsteps sounded behind him and he turned to find Grace carrying a pile of wood from the cottage. She placed it outside the building and turned to enter again. "What are you doing?" he called, approaching her.

She lifted her chin and dusted off her skirt. "I am cleaning my new home."

She was stubborn. He forced down his smile. She had put her golden curls up, at the back of her head and somehow that accented the soft lines of her face and jaw. She had long lashes, high cheekbones, and full lips. She moved to turn away and he called softly, "Grace. I will not force you to return. But your father's men will. I would say you have only a day before they arrive."

She turned to him, a troubled frown on her brow. "I have no desire to return."

"I don't think that matters to your father."

She glanced back at the cottage. "Let them come," she said in an unconvincing defiant voice. "I will never return." She turned to enter the cottage.

"Do you need help?"

She froze and stood that way for a moment. Then, she glanced over her shoulder at him. "You would help me?"

A curl of golden hair hung over her cheek and her blue eyes sparkled in the sunlight; a sheen of sweat made her brow glisten. Lord, she was beautiful! "It is my duty as a knight."

Confusion shone in her eyes as her gaze moved over him. She nodded. "You have a shovel," she stated. "You can start clearing the garden."

He watched her disappear into the cottage. For a moment, he debated what the use of clearing a garden she would never get to tend was. He sighed softly. It didn't matter. It would give him something to do. He removed his tunic and picked up the shovel.

William finished when the sun was just past noon. He wiped the sweat from his brow and surveyed his work. The weeds were gone, having been pulled and heaped into a pile. The ground had been turned over and prepared for the crop. If there was any. He couldn't imagine where Lady Grace was going to get seed. It wasn't a very big garden. If this was what the Mortain family had been paying a tithe on, it was amazing they hadn't starved.

"It looks good. The land looks fresh and ready for the seeds."

He didn't turn to know she stood just behind him. He nodded.

She handed him a flask.

He was pleased to see she had been drinking. She probably got it from Mortain's steed. He had seen her come out to the horse once during the day. He took it and drank deeply. It was not the best ale, but he was thirsty and it didn't matter. He handed it back to her and noticed the dark rings beneath her eyes. "You should not overwork yourself. It's been a long week for you."

She looked at him with those large, blue eyes.

Even with the dark rings shadowing her eyes, his

heart missed a beat. Strange. Her hair was unkempt with fly-away strands blowing gently in the wind; half of it had fallen from the tie she had put it up with. There was a smudge of dirt on her cheek. Her dress was a mess. One sleeve was ripped from the elbow to the wrist and the front of the blue gown was smeared with mud. He was stunned that through all of that he still thought she was the most beautiful woman he had ever seen. It was fitting she wanted nothing to do with him. More penance, he thought and looked at the garden again. "What were you going to plant?"

She laughed softly, a chuckle that sounded strangled. "I hadn't thought that far ahead. I guess the idea was better than the reality."

"As so happens with many things," William agreed. He put the shovel over his shoulder and walked to the side of the cottage. "It's going to rain. I will put the horses in the cottage with you tonight."

"Where will you sleep?"

"The tree will offer me enough shelter. I shall be fine there." He put the shovel down and turned to her. "I have bread. Are you hungry?"

She nodded and a strand of her golden hair fell forward over her cheek. She brushed it aside. "We can eat inside. I found two chairs sturdy enough to sit in."

He returned to Hellfire and picked up the two bags at his hooves and followed her into the cottage. He was surprised at how clean the small dwelling was. She had removed the broken furniture and swept the floors, removing the mattress. It was almost presentable. Two chairs were positioned near the cold hearth. He had half expected the room to be as it was when he had arrived. She had actually done a lot of work. It would have made a fine home. For someone. She sat in one of the chairs, he the other. He removed a loaf and handed it to her.

She took a bite. They ate quietly. "Will they come tomorrow?" she asked after she had swallowed. "My father's men."

"At the earliest, yes. If they followed the clues I did. If not it could be later, but they will come."

She silently ate her bread, chewing thoughtfully.

William didn't want to distress her, but he knew she was going home. One way or the other. Her father's men would not dally with her as he was. They would haul her on a horse and be off for the castle within minutes of finding her.

"You said it was your duty as a knight to help me."

He swallowed a bite of the bread. "I will not raise my sword against your father's men."

"I would not ask you to. That would only lead to your death. But if I asked you to help me, you would be bound by your duty as a knight."

He narrowed his eyes. What was the little imp up to? "It would depend what you asked me to do."

"Would you help me escape my marriage to you?"

CHAPTER NINE

William stared into Grace's amazing blue eyes for a long moment. He wasn't shocked by her request, but he was surprised she had asked him to help her. How could he condemn her to a marriage with him? His mission had been to bring her back to her father. He looked away from her. Knowing she did not want to marry him, he would never condemn her to a life with him. "Have you spoken to your father?"

"Of course. He is insistent that I marry you. He wishes to honor his vow to your father to combine the lands."

A vow and an increase in lands were both good reasons to marry. "And that is not important to you?"

Grace sighed. "Of course it is important. But... I think there is more to his request."

"What do you mean?"

She picked at the bread for a moment delicately, thoughtfully. The light from the setting sun showered in through the open door, casting a golden glow over her. "I can't explain it. My father loves me." But there

59

was no conviction in her voice. "He wants what is best for me. And yet, somehow I feel this is a punishment."

A punishment. Marriage to him was a punishment for her. Of course it was. Why would a woman as beautiful as Grace need to marry a knight without a future?

She wasn't looking at him. She gazed at the bread without really seeing it.

A punishment for what? Maybe she had it wrong. Maybe she didn't understand her father was telling the truth when he said she would marry him to combine the lands. Maybe... Then realization swept over him. Perhaps her father knew of her relationship with Sir Curtis and didn't approve. "You loved Sir Curtis."

"No!" Grace objected. "No. We were friends. He had agreed to help me escape."

William took a thoughtful bite from the small loaf of bread in his hand. He chewed quietly. A punishment for what? What could she have done to merit a futureless life with him? "Perchance your father thought there was more to it."

"More than friendship?"

William nodded. "And he disapproved."

She shook her head. "I don't think he cared who I was friends with. He never asked me. All that was important to him was his vow and gaining lands. Not my happiness."

There was something sad in her words, some underlying tension between her father and her that was obviously bothering her. "Women are often not consulted in their betrothal."

Grace looked down at the bread in her hands, shaking her head. A scowl marred her brow. "I never want to see him again," she whispered and tore a piece off.

Surprise rocked him. Her own father. She never wanted to see her father again. He saw the sheen of tears in her eyes and was shocked. His surprise gave way to anger. "Did he hurt you?"

She didn't look up. "He was my father," she said quietly. "Why would he hurt me?"

The question was directed at herself as much as him. She looked fragile and frightened. A sudden image of Lord Alan raising an angry fist and Grace cowering before him flashed in William's mind. His jaw tightened. He knew some men kept their women in line with a stern fist and an occasional beating, a philosophy he had never agreed with. "Did he hit you?"

Grace shook her head but didn't look at him.

He didn't know if he believed her. And it wasn't his place to ask.

Grace's shoulders drooped and her head bowed.

William had the sudden urge to take her in his arms and comfort her, to hold her. But he knew she would only pull away from his touch. Instead, he reached to her and placed a comforting hand on her wrist. "At some time you must face him, face your future."

She snapped her gaze to him and there was accusation in her eyes. "Have you faced your future?"

William closed himself off from the sudden, unexpected pain her angry words aroused in him. He slowly removed his hand. He had no right to touch her. "Yes. I know what my future holds." There was nothing for him. Just penance and a loveless life. No woman would have him. And he deserved none. He didn't even hope any more. He tried to live his life honorably after the death of the archbishop. He prayed every night and attended mass when he could. But he lived under no illusion. He knew there was no forgiveness for him.

"And you are content with it?" Grace wondered.

"I have accepted my fate."

She took a bite of bread and stared into the fire with resolve. "I will not accept mine. I am asking for your help."

"Your father will betroth you to another."

"He will not be cursed, will he?" She lifted her chin stubbornly.

Surprised at her sharp, hurtful words, he looked away. No. There were only three other men who could understand what he felt and what he was combating. "As you wish, m'lady. I will do all I can to help you break our betrothal."

William had given Grace a blanket for the evening and she curled up in it. One of the first things she had done when cleaning was to make a spot to sleep. It wasn't as comfortable as her chambers at the castle, but it wasn't filled with bugs. She had to admit William was more attentive than Curtis ever was. He saw to her comfort, her hunger. And he was honorable, which truthfully surprised her. He had agreed to help her prevent his own marriage to her.

For that, she was grateful.

She must have dozed off because the next thing she knew, a large trembling boom shook the ground. She leapt up in a panic. Curtis's horse whinnied and stomped its foot. William's horse remained calm, gazing out the door. Rain pelted the ground outside the doorway of the cottage in an onslaught of large, hard drops. It was raining. Not just raining, storming!

William was outside, caught in the thick of it!

She stepped forward, her hands stretched out in the darkness so she wouldn't bump into anything. The blanket slid off her shoulders. The blackness inside the cottage was so complete, she couldn't see anything.

Another flash of lightning lit the room and she used the flash of light to quickly make her way to the door. The heavy rain pelted the earth like a sheet of water, making it difficult to see in the distance. She looked at the tree where William had been sleeping, but couldn't see anything except shadows of trees swaying in the wind, their branches bending like fingers. "Sir William!" she called. Her heart pounded like the thunder. Her gaze swept the surroundings. "Sir William!" He was probably soaked through.

A forked tongue of light split the sky and she winced. She stepped out into the downpour, searching desperately. "William!" A loud crack of thunder erupted over her head and she cried out. The storm was alive with anger.

A shadowy figure stood from beneath a tree.

Rain drenched her as she stared at the shadow, not sure whether it was Curtis coming back from the grave to punish her or William. The man's figure approached slowly. She pushed wet strands of hair from her forehead so she could see. As the figure advanced slowly, she pressed her back to the wall of the cottage.

"What are you doing out here?"

Relief swept her. It was William, not some dead corpse rising, not some shadow monster, not a bandit. Just William. "It's raining pretty hard. I thought you'd rather be inside," she called loudly over the downpour.

He gently urged her back inside the cottage and followed her. He swept past her to his horse. "You couldn't sleep?"

"No," she said softly. Thunder boomed again over their heads, shaking the small structure. She looked up at the thatched roof, half expecting it all to come down around their heads.

William moved to the hearth. He fumbled around for a moment before a small fire jumped to life. "Come. Warm yourself."

Grateful for the light and the warmth, Grace did not need to be told again. She moved to the hearth and held out her hands, relishing the heat emanating from the fire. She knelt before the hearth.

He rose and moved back to his horse. When he returned, he draped a blanket over her shoulders.

She pulled it tight around her. They sat in silence for a long time. "He's a beautiful horse," Grace said. "What's his name?"

William chuckled and it was a low rolling sound that moved through her body and made her smile. "Hellfire."

"Why did you name him that? Such a beautiful

animal deserves a more majestic name."

"Because when he was young he was rather...stubborn and obstinate. Now..." He let the sentence hang.

"Now he's not?" she asked.

"I was going to say now it's appropriate."

Hellfire. A fitting name that tied well with William's future. Again, silence settled between them. A crack of thunder rocked the ground. Grace knew the tale. Everyone knew the tale. He and three of his friends had killed Archbishop Thomas Becket. The four knights had all proclaimed it was ordered by the king, but King Henry denied any knowledge of it. They were all excommunicated by Pope Alexander III. That was years ago. She had lost track of what had happened to the murderers. Until her father proclaimed she was to marry one. The darkness spread between them. Even the thunder was quiet. "Are you scared?"

"Of the thunder and lightning?" William asked.

"No. Of the afterlife. Of what it holds for you."

A long silence lingered between them; even the storm seemed to quiet to hear his answer. The fire in the hearth snapped and popped. "I'd be a fool to say no."

Grace pulled the blanket around her shoulders as another quake of thunder rumbled over their heads. She felt sorry for him. He certainly wasn't the image of the monster who killed the archbishop she had fashioned in her mind when she had first heard the tale.

"Thank you for allowing me cover inside. When the rain stops, I shall return outside."

He was so honorable. So thoughtful. It was hard to imagine him wielding a sword in a cathedral to kill a man of the cloth. She looked at him. He stared into the fire, the glow of the flames casting his face in a red hue. He was clean shaven with a square, strong jaw. His nose was straight. His eyes reflected the fire light of the hearth with a dark intensity. Dark wet strands of hair hung around his face. He was handsome, she would give him that. Thunder boomed overhead and she cast her gaze to the ceiling. The rain pounded the roof. She looked at him again and realized she would feel safer if he stayed in the darkness with her. It was a silly thought. After his hard work and kind treatment of her, she felt obligated to treat him civilly. Even if he did kill Curtis. Although she knew in her heart he had not. She wanted to blame him for her friend's death, but she knew Curtis had fallen on his own dagger. She had seen it with her own eyes. It had not been William's sword that had pierced him. "You are not what I expected."

William turned his head to look at her. "What did you expect?"

Embarrassed, Grace gazed into the fire. A small smile touched her lips. "Horns. Definitely glowing eyes." She clasped her hands and her grin faded. "I suppose I expected a man more like my father. A man who would not listen to me. A selfish man filled with hate. A terrible, cold man who wanted to grow his stature and combine the lands regardless of all else."

William was silent for a long time, until he asked, "What else is there?"

"Kindness. Love. I used to think God until my prayers went unanswered." She stood and prepared to move to her small corner to sleep.

He reached out and clasped her hand. "Don't give up on God, Lady Grace. His timeline is different than yours or mine."

Strange that he should still believe in a God that had given up on him. She eased her hand from his. "You may remain inside," she proclaimed.

He looked at her, shocked.

"If you'd like," she quickly added. "We can sleep across the room from each other." When she looked at him, she saw the confusion in his eyes. A smile spread across her lips. "I can't have the knight who is to aid me weakened and chilled by the storm."

"I assure you a storm will not weaken me."

She lifted her chin, regally. "But the ground will be wet and cold."

He nodded in agreement. "Aye. That it will. I would appreciate staying inside. I thank ye. I will sleep by the door."

Grace clasped her hands before her and turned away. She stopped and took a deep breath. "I'm sorry, Sir William."

"Sorry?"

Grace bowed her head and turned back to him. "I was angry and lashed out at you. I know you did not kill Curtis. I'm sorry for accusing you." When the silence stretched, she looked at him and caught the surprise in his eyes which made the guilt lurch forward in her heart.

Shock gave way to gratitude. "Thank you."

His modesty was daunting. And attractive. She nodded, her gaze sweeping over his fire-kissed face. The red light accented his perfect nose, his sensual lips, the warmth in his eyes. She found it strange that she liked the way he looked at her, that his company was so comforting. It was all strange. Because this was not the way she had ever felt with Curtis.

A mumbling from outside caused Grace to stir. She turned over, pulling the blanket over her shoulder. It was a moment before she realized the mumbling was muted talking. She sat up and stretched. Again, she heard the sound of communication. She couldn't make out the words, but she could hear the different tones and knew it was two men speaking. She threw the blanket from her legs and stood, moving quickly into the shadows. Had her father found her so soon? The cottage had only one opening for a door, but some of the planks near the front of the building were separating. She moved to them and bent down slightly to peer between the slots. She twisted her head, trying to see all around. In the front of the building, she spotted a man she did not know. He had dark hair and a thick beard. He wore commoners clothing of breeches and tunic. He was saying something to someone else, someone she assumed was William. The man nodded and moved away. She watched him go, tingles dancing along the nape of her neck as she craned her head for another glimpse of the man. Who was he? A man sent by her father? Or just some innocent farmer? She couldn't be too careful.

William entered the cottage. He looked around the room and took the reins of his horse. "Stay inside," he said softly to her. He led the horse outside.

His order worried her. There was something in his tone, a warning perhaps. Before she could ask about the man, William had departed.

She bent back to the parted wood and watched as William returned to the spot where he had been speaking to the man, Hellfire in tow. William began to tend to Hellfire. He lifted one of the horse's hooves and inspected it. He let the leg go and patted Hellfire's neck. William returned inside. "He's still out there. Stay inside." He picked up a bag and walked outside to his horse.

Again, Grace looked through the planks at the forest and the area all around. She couldn't see the man. Maybe William was mistaken, but she doubted it. He was a trained knight and he would know if someone was still lurking around. Who was the man? What did he want? She could only guess he was a scout sent by her father. William did say they would come today. But it couldn't be her father's man because William would have handed her over. There would be no reason to hide from him. She watched William tend Hellfire. He cleaned the horse's shoes, removing small rocks and debris. He checked the animal's legs and body. Then he tied Hellfire to a tree, letting him eat the grass.

William removed his sword from its scabbard. He looked down the long length and then sat down. He took a whetstone from his saddle bag and began to sharpen his weapon.

Grace scanned the surrounding forest, but still did not see the man. Why would he be hiding? To see what William was doing? Because he didn't believe whatever William had told him? She straightened, struggling to fight back her apprehension. Who was that man? What did he want? She bent and looked out through the planks again. William was still sharpening his sword. Hellfire was still eating grass. The man was nowhere in sight.

She needed to do something to distract herself from her nervousness. She rose up away from the loose planks and moved deeper into the cottage. She pulled the blanket from the bed and folded it, preparing it for the inevitable journey back to the castle. She took one of William's bags from the floor and opened it to put the blanket inside. She paused. On the top of his clothing and supplies was a crucifix. She picked it up and looked at it. It was made of gold with the image of Jesus on it. The expression on the statue's face was of Jesus crying out and looking skyward. She ran her finger over the figure's face. It was beautiful. Whoever had made it had taken a lot of time and effort, and even love, to mold it.

Footsteps made her look toward the door. William entered. When he spotted her, his gaze shifted to the crucifix. His face darkened; his brows furrowed. He marched to her side.

Grace tried to explain, "I was putting the blanket away. I didn't mean --"

He snatched the crucifix from her hands and shoved it back into the bag. He stood over her for a long moment, his face tight and angry, his jaw clenched.

Grace waited for the yelling, waited for the barrage of harsh words he would use to berate her. She had experienced such rage many times from her father and expected no different from him.

Instead, he whirled without a word and stalked from the cottage.

CHAPTER TEN

William tossed the bag down in the area where he had been sharpening his blade. What was she doing going through his personal items? She had no right! He sat down and picked up the stone to run it along his blade. His movements were quick and intense. The fact she was going through his bag wasn't really the reason he was so angry, he knew. It was the sight of her small hands holding that cross. That golden cross. He had cleaned it, of course. Many times. But he knew he could never get all the blood from it. And Grace had been holding it. Her innocent, delicate hands had held it reverently. Reverently. He glanced down at the golden cross, into the unseeing eyes he had stared at a hundred times. He had found the cross covered in blood in a temple in Jerusalem after a huge battle. It had been a massacre and many on both sides had lost their lives. But the cross had survived. It was a reminder of all he had endured, all he had done. It had been Hugh de Morville who came up beside him when he was holding the bloody cross in his hands. Hugh had looked at the cross for a long moment and then glanced at William. Something had passed between the two of them in that look. They were brothers. Brothers in all ways except blood.

Hugh was a good man, perhaps a bit overly ambitious at the time, eagerly wanting to gain the king's favor. But weren't they all? William thought of the night again, that night that had forever changed his destiny, wishing he had a chance to do it over again.

They were donning their armor, as if to go to war. Reginald was insistent the armor was needed. "The monks will protect him. We don't have a choice."

"They are defenseless!" Hugh exclaimed. "What kind of knights are we if we cannot overpower a man of the cloth?"

"There are many of them and only four of us," Richard le Brey said. "We will use whatever force we must to take the archbishop to King Henry."

"Aye!" Reginald agreed.

William glanced at Hugh. He read the concern in Hugh's eyes. William often wondered if he could have stopped it with Hugh's help. Hugh began to put on his armor. Richard followed his movement. Only William hesitated. They didn't need armor to overcome the archbishop. He didn't like it. He put a hand on Reginald's arm. "No harm will come to Becket."

Reginald jerked his arm free of William's hold. "We will take him by force, if need be. But he will return to Henry." He held out his hand. "Are you with us?"

William glanced from Richard to Hugh and then back to Reginald. These men were his friends. They had all hatched this plan together. He would not abandon them now. He nodded and clasped Reginald's arm. "With you."

A grin spread across Reginald's lips.

"Quickly, sirs!" A monk raced out of the doors of the hall toward them. His cold breath formed a puff with each breath he took. He pushed his hood from his head. "He has escaped into the cathedral! This way!"

The four knights finished putting on their armor and followed the monk toward the cathedral. The wooden doors were closing as they approached and the monk came up short, stopping on the stairs to the cathedral. The four knights raced by him and shoved at the large wooden doors.

At first, there was resistance and William pushed as hard as he could. Then, the doors swung open. As they entered, a group of monks fled to the side wall. They had been trying to keep the doors shut to prevent them from entering the cathedral.

"King's men!" Reginald shouted as he entered. His voice echoed through the large vaulted room.

At the front of the church, monks crowded together around the altar. As the four knights made their way toward the altar, William noticed even more monks had gathered in groups along the side walls, all of them cowering in fear.

The four knights approached the altar.

"Where is Thomas Becket, traitor to the king?" Reginald demanded.

The monks near the altar remained silent, fearful. They clung to each other.

As the knights approached, moving past statues of saints and angels filling the cathedral, William saw the statue of the Virgin Mary on one side of the altar. She watched with cold eyes, her arms outstretched. Imploring. On the other side of the altar was a statue of Saint Benedict. Two large pillars stood at either side of the altar.

"Where is the archbishop?" Reginald called, his voice

echoing forcefully through the cathedral.

Thomas Becket emerged from behind a group of monks, easing them gently aside as if they were part of a human barricade trying to protect him. "Here I am, not a traitor to the king but a priest. Here I am, ready to suffer in the name of He who redeemed me with His blood. God forbid that I should flee on account of your swords or that I should depart from righteousness."

"Absolve and restore to communion those you have excommunicated and return to office those who have been suspended!" Richard ordered.

Mumblings grew louder near the door where the monks cowered. A large group had gathered there. Hugh quickly raced to them, brandishing his sword before them to discourage any interference from them.

The archbishop shook his head, lifting his chin. "No penance has been made, so I will not absolve them."

William knew Richard was specifically speaking of the Bishops of London and Salisbury. The archbishop had excommunicated them for their support of the king. A wave of righteousness crested inside of William. The defiance in the archbishop's tone, even in the face of the king's wrath angered him. No man was above the king's authority.

Richard pulled his sword from its sheath.

"If you do not do as the king commands, then you will die," Reginald threatened.

William should have left at that point. He had never intended to kill the archbishop. Excommunicated for good intentions. It almost made him smile. But there was nothing to smile about. An innocent man was dead. As the Pope had ordered as part of his penance, William had spent fourteen years fighting in Jerusalem, fourteen long bloody years. He still didn't feel forgiven. Even though his penance was almost over. Nothing could absolve him for his part in the archbishop's death. Not all the Muslim blood in the world could ever make it right. After so much death and battle, he realized he could never be absolved. Not for Becket's death. Not for all the death he had delivered. The cross was a reminder of the blood on his hands. He closed the bag.

He ran the stone across the blade of his weapon. He would not have another innocent death on his hands. He had no intention of letting Grace be harmed. He had to get her out of there. He glanced into the forest. The trees swayed in a breeze, the leaves rustling. He couldn't see him, but he knew Peter was still out there. The man was not going to give up. They would have to make a run for it.

William stood and returned to the cottage.

Grace whirled from the cold hearth. A beam of light from a portion of broken roof shone in and fell upon her, bathing her in a heavenly light.

He froze. Her eyes were large and blue, twinkling in the sunlight. His gaze dropped to her full lips. Even with the dirt on her face and her riotous waves of tumbling blonde curls hanging about her face, she was beautiful. He couldn't move for a long moment. He swallowed in a dry throat.

She stepped forward, clasping her hands before her. "I'm sorry. I shouldn't have gone through your belongings. I was just putting the blanket --"

"It doesn't matter," he answered in a gruff voice. He cleared his throat and looked away, searching the ground for some semblance of rationality. "We will have to leave quickly. Prepare yourself. I will bring

Hellfire in." He looked at her again. His thought vanished beneath the stare of her gaze. "Be ready." He turned away.

"Are we in danger?"

He paused. He didn't want to alarm her, but he didn't want to lie. "Yes," he answered. He left the cottage and picked up the bags, slinging them casually over his shoulder. He whistled softly as he led Hellfire in, secretly scanning the forest. William didn't see him, but he knew Peter was out there. Watching. Waiting. The questions Peter had asked about Grace made it obvious he was tracking her. He knew the man, had worked with him before. And he didn't like him. Peter was unscrupulous and untrustworthy.

Once William entered the cottage, he began to load Hellfire. Grace helped, handing him another bag. William put the saddle on his horse, murmuring softly to Hellfire. When the task was complete, he straightened and looked at Grace. She stared at him, concern furrowing her forehead. He put the saddle on the other horse. He would use Curtis's horse to confuse Peter by sending the animal down another road. When he was finished, he turned to Grace and stretched out a hand to her.

She looked down at it. "Perhaps you should go without me."

He lowered his hand.

"You are a good knight. Much different than I expected. I don't want you hurt because of me."

He lifted his hand to her again. "I will not leave without you."

She looked at him and he could have swore there

was admiration in her eyes. But that couldn't be. Admiration was not a look people bestowed on him, especially not beautiful noble women. She placed her hand into his. The touch of her warm skin sent a rush through his body. He pulled her gently forward and caught her by the waist. For a moment, he looked down at her. Lord, how he wanted to kiss her lips. They stood that way for a long moment. His gaze moved over her face, caressing every curve. She was beautiful. He had been unprepared for these feelings. And for Grace. He was unworthy of her. He lifted her onto Hellfire. "We'll have to ride quickly." He put his foot into the stirrup and mounted behind her. He tied the reins of Mortain's horse to his pommel and reached around her to take up Hellfire's reins. "Are you ready?"

She nodded, wrapping one hand around the pommel of the saddle and one around one of his arms.

He urged Hellfire forward, and the other horse matched pace. Then he spurred his horse hard into a full out gallop. He charged down the road. He heard a whoosh and bent low over Grace, trying to protect her. He was certain it had been an arrow. Anger rose up in William. A man looking to bring a kidnapped woman back to the castle would not be firing arrows at her. There was much more going on here than met the eye. He kicked Hellfire, urging his steed faster. Faster. His fingers masterfully clutched the reins, maneuvering the horse from side to side, making it harder for the arrows to find their mark. The only positive thing that could come from the existence of arrows was that arrows meant a bow, and a bow meant Peter was most likely standing somewhere, aiming. Peter would have to mount his horse and give chase. Those few moments would give them time to escape. Precious little time, but better than nothing.

William pushed Hellfire on. The two horses charged down the road, quickly reaching a junction where the road split in two. He untied Mortain's horse and urged him down the road leading to Willoughby Castle before steering Hellfire down the other fork.

Grace watched Curtis's horse ride away. "Do you think it will work?"

William hoped so, but he was taking no chances. "I don't know."

As they turned a bend in the road, William had to swerve Hellfire to avoid a farmer with a cart full of cabbages who shouted angrily after him. Hellfire stumbled and almost fell, but righted himself.

William kept up the pace, listening to hear if the farmer shouted again. That would mean Peter was giving chase. But as he listened, the shout never came. Still, William did not relent. The more distance they put between them and the bowman, the better. And William knew Peter would not give up.

After traveling for a good time at a quick pace, the clouds parted and the sun beat down on them from almost directly over head. William turned Hellfire off of the main road.

"Where are we going?" Grace asked.

"I'm hoping that the man will follow Mortain's horse toward Willoughby Castle. That's where he'll expect us to go. He may even be riding ahead to cut us off."

"We're not going to Willoughby Castle?"

"Not yet. There's a stream up here. It flows into the river Bovey."

She twisted in the saddle to look at him. "Bovey?"

William stared into the distance, toward the town of Bovey. "I'm hoping this will throw him off of our trail. We're going to my home."

Grace finally relaxed when William slowed Hellfire and guided him through the water at a walk. She glanced over her shoulder, taking in the surrounding forest. "Is he gone?"

"Not for good," William answered. There was a certainty in his tone that made Grace nervous. "We've distanced ourselves from him and with any luck lost him. But he will be back. He won't give up."

"What does he want?"

"You. He was looking for you."

"To bring me back," Grace answered solemnly.

William glanced behind them for a moment before twisting to face forward. "How well did you know Sir Curtis?"

She scowled, considering his question. "He was a friend. He worked at my father's castle for years. Why do you ask?"

William was silent for a long moment.

Grace twisted to look back at him.

His blue eyes were focused intently on a point in front of them. "We talked about ransom. Remember I told you you were lucky? He could have killed you."

Grace nodded. She remembered his words. He had been trying to figure out why Curtis would have brought her back to a place that was so easy to find.

William reached back and with a tug pulled something from one of the bags. He brought his fist forward and it was wrapped around an arrow shaft. "Apparently, that was exactly what he had in mind."

CHAPTER ELEVEN

Shock raced through Grace as she stared at the arrow William clutched in his hand. Curtis had wanted her dead? They were friends! She had known him all of her life! She trembled even as everything in her body rebelled at the prospect. "It can't be. Why do you say this?"

"I know that man who came to the cottage. He is a killer. He kills for coin. And not much of it."

Numbness and disbelief spread through Grace. She couldn't believe it. "Maybe my father hired him to bring me back."

"Your father has castle guards to bring you back. He would not have hired a man like him."

It just couldn't be. Curtis couldn't have wanted the coin. They were friends. She trusted him. He wanted her dead? It was too much to believe. "Sir Curtis was a knight bound by his oaths. He would not have hurt me."

"He wasn't going to."

Silence spread as Grace thought about William's

words. Curtis had eaten most of the food under the pretense of needing his strength to protect her. He had not taken very good care of her, nor had he remained with her to protect her. Nothing he had done made any sense. She had given him coin, under his direction, so they could escape. He had taken her to his old home, which turned out to be the exact place they would come to look for her. Would he have paid someone to kill her? Could William be right? She shook her head, still not believing Curtis was capable of something like that. She knew him. Or thought she did.

Distressed, disturbed, and unsure, she remained silent. Thoughts swirled through her mind. They had made plans of escape and a future together. But as she thought back on their journey, she realized he hadn't come up with the idea of running; she was the one who had thought of it. And he hadn't brought up the thought of their fantasy life together; she had asked him about it. He had told her once of his father's cottage, but she was the one who had decided they would live there. The only thing he had contributed was asking her to bring coin. She bowed her head. What a fool she was! She had been so blind, so eager to run away from a marriage to a knight who was damned that she had not seen the reality before her. She looked up at William, her thoughts returning to the man pursuing them. "Can you stop him?"

"I will see you back to your father safely," William proclaimed. There was no doubt in his voice, only fact.

She felt tears flood through her eyes, closing her throat. He would take her home. To her father. Back to another man who wanted nothing to do with her. Maybe in the face of her prolonged absence, her father's anger would calm. While she was at Bovey with William, perhaps her father would know she was safe and that would be enough for him. Perhaps. But she knew it wouldn't be. She had never been able to make him happy. Not him or any man. Not her father, not Curtis.

The horse moved from side to side beneath her as it walked. William's arms were around her, clutching the reins. "You needn't worry, Grace," William said softly. "I will protect you and see you safely home. The marriage will be dissolved and you will have everything you wanted."

Grace nodded and looked away. Yes. Everything she wanted, her mind repeated but there was doubt festering at the edge of her mind that made mockery of his words. Was she sure of what she wanted any more?

When William was convinced they were not being followed, they stopped near a stream in the forest. William gave her bread to eat and left her alone by the stream. She rinsed her hair and face and any exposed skin she could manage to reach without removing any clothing.

When she returned to their camp, the sun was setting. Dappled red light fell upon the ground. At first, she didn't see William and her stomach clenched in nervousness. Had he abandoned her? But as she stepped around a tree, she saw him on his knees. She inhaled in alarm, thinking at first he was hurt. Then she saw his folded hands and bowed head and realized he was praying. His dark hair fell over his strong shoulders. His powerful body was completely still. His eyes were closed.

The sight shocked her. A cursed knight was praying? To a God who didn't listen. The irony didn't escape her. She turned to go, but stopped. The golden rays of the sun touched his head and shoulders making a halo of gold. She couldn't take her gaze from him. She knew she was intruding and she should let him pray, but she couldn't move; she could only stare at the sight of the humbled knight on his knees. He was magnificent. So strong and so proud. And so amazingly handsome.

And cursed.

She felt a wave of sadness wash over her. She wished he wasn't cursed. She wished he hadn't killed the archbishop. She wished he had peace.

He took a deep breath and opened his eyes, locking gazes with her. He made the sign of the cross, touching his forehead, his stomach and each shoulder before standing.

Grace came forward. "I didn't mean to intrude."

"I was done."

"Do you pray every night?"

"I pray every chance I get."

It was the fact that he had never given up hope that sent another wave of sympathy through her. After everything that had happened to him, he still prayed. He moved by her. "Why did you do it?" she couldn't help asking. "Why did you kill Archbishop Becket?"

He stopped cold, his shoulders stiff. He gazed into the darkness of the forest for a long moment, almost as if remembering. Then, he slowly turned his head to her. His stunning blue eyes fastened on her. "I did it for my king." He narrowed his gaze slightly and continued past her.

There was something practiced and stiff in his speech. It was a rehearsed answer, she realized. Almost as if he had been asked so many times before that it was the only answer he could give. And it served its purpose, she realized. She had stopped asking about it.

William moved to Hellfire and opened a bag. He pulled the blankets out, handing them to her. "We can't light a fire, but you should be warm enough with these."

Grace took the blankets, unable to look away from him. So strong. So stoic. She felt confident he would protect her. But she had believed that about Curtis, too. "You didn't have to do this," she whispered, drawing his gaze. "You could have let my father's men return me to Willoughby Castle."

"Is that what you think of me? That I would leave you in the forest to fend for yourself until your father's men came?" His square jaw was tight; his blue eyes snapped flame. "I suppose you would think that. After all, I am the same man who killed the archbishop." He whirled away from her.

She stood, stunned. "Sir William!" she called. He halted, his shoulders rigid. "I meant no insult. I just thought... As my betrothed, you would be angry I ran away with another man."

"You were under a misguided assumption. You

were not running away with another man as much as running away from me. That, I can understand."

Again, she felt her heart twist with heartache. Running away from him? "William," she said, moving to his side. She reached out and touched his arm. The muscles beneath his tunic jumped at her touch. She didn't know what to say to him; she just knew she wanted to comfort him. "You are a very honorable knight."

He looked down at her. His hard eyes softened and he took her hand in his and pressed a kiss to her knuckles. "Thank you for thinking that." He held her hand for a moment longer before releasing it and turning away.

Grace stood, frozen. She stared at her hand. It tingled where his lips had brushed her skin. She ran her fingers over the spot. He had kissed her.

She was running through darkness. Long shadows reached for her. An ominous dark hand grabbed her skirt.

Grace jerked awake. Startled, unnerved, she glanced around. The surrounding forest was shaded in gray tones. It was night. She moved her legs, but her skirt caught on something. She pulled her legs away from the object and found the edge of her dress had snagged on the branch of a bush. She sighed and sat back. Something was stabbing her in the back. She brushed at the ground to find a stick had worked its way beneath her. She noticed one blanket was pulled over her waist, but the other lay uselessly aside. She must have thrown it off.

Instinctively, she looked across the camp to where William slept. He was in a sitting position, but she knew he was asleep because his head lulled to one side. She gathered the discarded blanket and rose, moving to him. She spread the blanket out and eased it up over his legs.

There was a sudden flash of movement. In the next second, his eyes were open, his sword tip pressed to her throat.

CHAPTER TWELVE

William stared into Grace's wide eyes. Through his groggy sleep, he had heard movement and reacted instinctively, grabbing his sword. He dropped the blade, horrified. "Grace." He leaned forward, taking her face in his hands. "Are you hurt? Did I--?" He inspected her neck, running his hand over her smooth skin to ensure there was no blood, no mark.

She shook her head.

He held her face in his hands, his thumbs sweeping over her cheeks. "I'm sorry, Grace," he whispered over and over. If he had hurt her, even by accident... His gaze swept her face, touching every inch of her soft skin, every curve. Lord, he had not meant to raise his weapon to her, to touch her warm skin with the cold blade. Alarm gripped his stomach in a tight knot of horror. All he wanted to do was make sure she was unhurt. All he wanted to do was touch her skin. All he wanted to do was kiss her lips. In a frenzy of concern and desperation, he leaned forward and pressed his lips to hers. Her mouth was soft. So soft and pliant. And warm.

She gasped softly beneath his kiss.

The spell was broken and he pulled back quickly as if she had scalded his skin. He opened his mouth, but no words came out. He was mortified at what he had done. He had no right to touch her, no right to take such loveliness against himself, no right to stroke his cursed lips against innocent ones. Even as he thought the thought, his gaze settled on her lips and desire engulfed him. He shot to his feet and retreated to the tree behind him as if to distance himself from the temptation she offered. "Forgive me, m'lady," he uttered, horrified at his audacity.

She stood, pressing her fingers to her lips, gazing at him.

He clenched his teeth and looked away. "Grace..." That was when he noticed the blanket on the ground. He looked up at her. She had come to give him the blanket. The simple gesture warmed his heart until he remembered he had greeted her with violence, almost cutting her neck. "You should stay on your side of the camp."

"You are not a danger to me."

He looked at her in disbelief. "I put a sword to your neck."

"You would not have harmed me." Her tone was confident.

Much more confident than he felt. He had seen so much blood, in the wars, in the death of the archbishop, at the hands of others, by his own hand. It was instinct for him to protect himself with a weapon. But he never wanted to raise a blade to her. "I don't want to. That's why you should stay on your side of the camp."

She dropped her chin as if in confusion.

He stepped toward her. "Grace. I promised to see you safely to your father. I intend to honor that vow."

She lifted her large eyes to him. They reflected the moon in their depths. And William knew he was in trouble. How could he resist her? Such beauty. Such innocence. But he had to. She did not want to marry him. And he had given his word to help her escape the betrothal. She was right. No woman in her right mind would want to be wife to him.

"You kissed me."

He gritted his teeth and looked down. What could he tell her? He would have to hurt her so she kept her distance from him. He would have to lie to her to keep them apart. "I thought you were someone else."

It worked. Her face fell; hurt shone in her vulnerable eyes before she turned away. Without a word, she moved back to her spot beneath the tree opposite of his. She lay down, keeping her back to him.

Guilt assailed William, but he knew this was better for them both. He would not be tempted to kiss her again. And she would not be tempted to be near him. Part of him was very sad at this prospect, but he knew it was the right decision. He turned and lay down, tucking his hands beneath his head to stare at the stars through the leaves of the tree. He reached down and pulled the blanket over his legs. Regret and remorse kept him from sleep. The only thing he managed to think of was a cottage and Grace to come home to.

'I thought you were someone else.' The words haunted Grace. Humiliation burned her cheeks. Hurt pierced her heart with a stinging sensation. She could barely look at William. Why? Why should it matter to her? She didn't want to marry him anyway! And yet, she could not stop thinking about his kiss. The urgent, desperate feel of his lips moving over hers. It was so unexpected, so... warm.

As they packed up the camp and she folded the blanket he had slept beneath, she wondered if he kissed her again would it be tender?

It didn't matter. He would never kiss her again and she should not want him to. She opened one of the bags to put the blanket inside. The golden cross tumbled out. She gasped, afraid William would be angry with her for going through his items again. She glanced over her shoulder at him across the camp. He was saddling Hellfire, tightening a cinch strap. Grace picked up the cross to put it back in the bag, but then she paused, staring down at the face. The face had been carved with such emotion, such heartbreak. The blank eyes gazed skyward, the mouth open as if crying out. She felt such anguish. She wondered if that was why William kept it. To remind him of his duty. Her thumb swept down the cross...and caught on a chip in its surface. It hadn't been there before, she was certain. She wondered briefly how it had gotten there, but quickly put the cross back into the bag and closed it, lest William catch her with it again. She picked up the bag and noticed a tear in the side. She put her finger in the hole, confused. It hadn't been ripped before. She straightened as realization struck her. The arrow! It must have hit the bag...and the cross.

"What is it?" William asked, moving toward her.

She spun and for a moment guilt settled over her. Then, she lifted her chin. She had done nothing wrong. "This tear. Is it where the arrow hit?"

William looked at the hole with a scowl and then back over at Hellfire. He nodded. "I believe so, yes. Why do you ask?"

Her mouth dropped slightly. "It was a miracle that it didn't hit Hellfire."

William grinned, taking the bag from her. "Well. I don't know if it was a miracle, but it certainly was luck."

The golden cross caught the blow of the arrow. It couldn't have been coincidence, could it? As William turned away from her, she stared at him. She had prayed for a knight to save her. A knight she could love. Could it be...? No. William was going to help her escape the betrothal. He was not the knight she had prayed for.

They rode toward Bovey. William's arms were around her, clutching the reins, almost holding her as he steered Hellfire. His arms were strong and secure and safe and comforting and... For a moment she allowed herself to be swept away into a daydream. William holding her tenderly, pressing his warm lips against hers.

Then she snapped herself out of her reverie. She

was a silly girl! She was a foolish girl! The men she wanted didn't want her. William was like Curtis and her father. She could not make him happy, any more than she could make Curtis or her father happy. And she shouldn't want to! He was a cursed man, his soul damned to the fires of hell! Still... She couldn't help but wonder if his soul was like that golden statue carved atop the cross. Anguished and crying out.

They came to the top of a small hill. Birds chirped in the blue skies above, men worked some of the land in the fields below. Small cottages dotted the landscape. Further in the distance, Grace could see a wall surrounding a town and manor home beside a river. She could only assume this was his home. This was Bovey Tracey.

He spurred Hellfire into a canter down the hill.

The sun was warm and welcoming and relief surged inside of Grace. They had made it to safety. A warm bed. Food. William's home.

They came to the bottom of the hill and William urged Hellfire forward with a gentle kick. The horse walked toward the town. The large wooden gates leading inside were open and William steered Hellfire through them. Merchants called out from open shop windows. The baker ran up to them with a basket of fresh bread. "Care to try a piece of bread? Baked fresh here just this morn!"

They continued past him. A child raced across the road before them, chasing a duck. Somewhere behind them, a woman called, "Paul!"

Before they reached the manor home, William stopped Hellfire before a small church. He dismounted and stood staring at the building for a long moment.

Grace looked up at the tall steeple. At the very top was a bell. William said he prayed whenever he could. He glanced back at her. Without a word, she stretched her arms to him. He assisted her dismount. Then, she took Hellfire's reins.

William grinned, taking the reins from her hand. "I won't leave you."

She hooked her hand through his arm. "Then we shall go in together."

William tethered Hellfire and they walked up the two steps to the church.

At the tall wooden double doors, William hesitated. Even though the doors were open in welcome, he was still excommunicated for his part in the murder of the archbishop. He glanced at Grace. She was looking at him with concern. He placed his hand comfortingly over Grace's where it lay on his arm, then took a small breath and entered the church.

Grace released his arm and entered one of the pews in the back and sat.

She wasn't praying. Interesting. He had thought she would. It wasn't his to say. William moved forward. It had been a long time since he had been here. The ceiling stretched far above his head. The same statue of St. Peter that had stared down at him in disapproval, still stared down at him with the same disapproval. It seemed nothing had changed. Nothing except him. He stopped in the middle of the aisle, before the altar and fell to his knees. It mattered not that the ground was cold and hard. It was not even close to the punishment he deserved. After he had given his devotion, he stood, expecting an explosion of thunder or the walls to bleed.

From deeper in the church, a voice called, "William! Boy, is that you?"

Father John appeared from the rear of the altar, hobbling toward him. He was not the man William remembered. He had aged heavily since the last time William had seen him. He used the pews as support to approach. William moved forward to greet him. He held out his hand.

Father John grabbed his arm and yanked him into a tight embrace. "Boy, it is good to see you."

"And you, Father," William said, relaxing in the old man's hold. His past returned in the father's arms. For a moment, it was as if he had never left. He was transported to the boy he had been. A mischievous youngster, he used to play tricks on Father John whenever he got a chance. Usually, moving items around on the altar when he wasn't looking. He suspected Father John knew who was doing it, but the father never gave up the belief that it was the Holy Spirit.

William pulled back to look at him. One eye was glossy white. Wrinkles lined his face. Most of his hair was gone and the remainder had turned white. But, his smile was genuine. "How are things, Father?"

"Nothing ever changes in Bovey Tracey," Father John said.

William had to smile at that. He had noticed differences in the town that made him feel like a stranger. "Is Ralph in residence?"

"No. Not for years. Steward Thomas is here."

William nodded. He had never met Steward Thomas. "Can you get a message to Lord Alan for me?"

"Lord Alan?" Father John pondered the question with a scowl, glancing at Grace in the rear of the church. "Yes. Yes. I could have the blacksmith's son run a message to Willoughby Castle. Get me the message when you can."

"The blacksmith's *son*?" William ran a hand of disbelief through his hair. "I can't believe any woman would have the patience to deal with Bruno."

"She's an angel, that's for sure!"

William laughed and lay a hand on Father John's shoulder. "I'll have Luke run it over to you later today. Luke is still here, isn't he?"

Father John scowled and pursed his lips. "He reminds me of you when you were young. Headstrong and disobedient."

"Me?" William asked in disbelief. "I was always the ideal student."

Father John's roar of laughter shook the church.

It was the laugh William remembered. He was home. And he had missed Father John who had always been a friend to him.

Slowly, his laughter faded and Father John elbowed him. "Who is she?" He indicated Grace with a jerk of his chin.

William glanced at Grace where she sat in the pew looking at the rafters and the statues in the church. Her hair hung around her shoulders in a disarray of gold. Her brows lifted up as she inspected the building. "Lady Grace of Willoughby," William answered. "Come. I will introduce you."

Father John nodded and followed William down the aisle. "Emily will be delighted to see you."

"Emily?"

"Your cousin Emily is here for a week. I'm sure you'll be happy about that."

William detected a note of wry humor in his tone. Emily. He hadn't seen her for years, but what he remembered was a bubbly young girl, full of life. She always managed to draw him into her world, as he was her favorite cousin. As William approached Grace, she stood up. He took her hand, gathering her to his side. "Lady Grace, this is Father John."

Father John bowed his head. "It's a pleasure to meet you, Lady Grace."

"And you, Father John," Grace said with a smile. "How long have you known William?"

Father John rumbled with a laugh. "Since the dawn of time."

"I didn't know he was that old."

"When you have time, I will tell you some stories about William. He wasn't always such an outstanding man."

William groaned softly. No, he hadn't always been good. He dreaded, good-naturedly, the stories Father John would tell.

"I would love it," Grace admitted.

"How long are you staying?" Father John asked.

"I don't know," William admitted.

Father John placed his hands on William's shoulders. "It is always good to see you, boy." He embraced him tightly.

William was startled at first but then returned the

hug warmly.

Father John released William and looked at Grace. "A pleasure to meet you, Lady Grace."

William led Grace from the church. He took Hellfire's reins and glanced at Grace. She was looking up at the top of the church. William followed her gaze.

She pointed upward.

William stared at the sky and then at the top of the church. It was a single small tower, the same as he remembered from his childhood. "I don't see anything."

"The church spire is leaning."

At last William saw what she was looking at. It was true, the top of the point was leaning westward. "So it is."

"It should be fixed."

"Aye," William agreed. "It should be." He took her hand and led her toward the manor home.

They were greeted and welcomed by Steward Thomas. He was a tall man, very thin. He put off a capable and responsible demeanor. As he led them inside the manor home and down a corridor, he spoke with William about the tallies and the harvest. William half listened. He cast a sideways glance at Grace to see her gazing at the tapestries hanging on the walls. He followed her gaze, unimpressed by the representations of the coronation of King William she was staring at. He supposed he had never paid them much attention, but Grace seemed fascinated by each one.

"William!"

William turned at the familiar voice to find Emily

racing toward them. Her blonde hair hung in perfect ringlets; her green kirtle swung about her legs as she moved forward. She was no longer the child he remembered.

She stopped just before him, a scowl on her brow. "Did you think to sneak home without greeting me?"

He recognized her play-angry ploy immediately. Apparently, she hadn't grown up all that much. He dropped his chin. "How could I do that?" He opened his arms and she jumped into them, wrapping her hands around him. He squeezed her and placed a hearty kiss on her cheek.

Emily pulled back to gaze into William's eyes. Her bright brown orbs shone with joy as she stared at him. "You'd best not," she warned. "I would be devastated."

William indicated Grace. "This is Lady Grace of Willoughby Castle. Grace, this is my cousin, Emily."

Emily turned to Grace, and after a quick perusal, her face lit with excitement. "How wonderful to meet you!"

William had no doubt that Emily would relish having another female in the manor home to gossip with. "We shan't be here long, Em," William warned. "I am escorting Lady Grace home to Willoughby Castle."

"Oh pshh," Emily murmured, waving him off. "Lady Grace shall stay as long as she wants!" She clasped Grace's arm tightly. "We are going to be the very best of friends, I can tell!"

William was pleased to see the grin on Grace's lips. He shrugged helplessly as Emily pulled Grace down the hallway. He wasn't at all certain whether this alliance was going to be good for him or bad.

CHAPTER THIRTEEN

Upon Emily's insistence, Steward Thomas gave Grace the room next to her. William was across the hall from them. He was glad to see Emily again. He retired to his room to change his dusty riding clothes. He began to lift his tunic over his head when Emily rushed into his room. William cast her a wry look as he pulled his tunic back into place. "Ever the same, I see."

Emily chuckled and threw herself onto the bed. "Who is she? She is absolutely lovely."

William had to agree. Grace was beautiful. But he would never admit that to Emily. She had a way of interfering. He walked to the bed where his bags and belt lay. "I introduced you."

Emily peered at him through squinted eyes. "What aren't you telling me?"

William sighed. He knew she would find out eventually. She would simply ask him and Grace repeatedly until one of them couldn't stand it a moment longer and told her. He would never subject

Grace to Emily's annoying persistence. He loved Emily, but she could be like a gnat infesting a wound. He turned to look at her. She lay across the bed, resting her chin on the palms of her hands, gazing at him with a smirk. Her brown eyes twinkled. "You already know, don't you?" he asked.

She teetered a small laugh. "Of course! You can't let her get away." She rolled onto her back, her arms outstretched, staring at the ceiling. "Oh, William! A chance at a normal life for you. Children!"

William took a deep breath and sat beside her. A normal life. He could never have a normal life. Not him. "She doesn't want to marry me."

Emily gasped and sat up. "She must not know you! Any woman would be lucky to have you as a husband."

"Not every woman sees it that way," he said quietly.

Emily took his hand into her own. "God has forgiven you. You must forgive yourself. Perhaps this is a new start --"

William pulled his hand free of her hold. "There is no forgiveness for me."

"You mustn't talk like that, William," Emily said softly. "There is forgiveness for everyone."

"Everyone doesn't murder the archbishop."

Emily sighed softly. "It wasn't your idea." She caught his hand again and clasped it tightly. "These are not the hands of a murderer."

"I didn't finish him, but I was a part of it. Don't make light of it, Em. I'm as guilty as the rest."

"Maybe Lady Grace was sent to you as a sign of forgiveness."

William shrugged. "Regardless. I won't force her to marry me. I've given my word to help her escape the betrothal."

Emily cocked her head to the side and her eyes twinkled in that familiar way. She was up to something. "We'll just see about that."

"Emily," William growled in a warning tone. "I don't want you to get involved in this. This is between me and Grace."

"Of course!" Emily protested and stood. "When have I ever become involved in one of your affairs?"

"When haven't you?" He could count at least five times without thinking about it.

"That was when I was younger. I haven't seen you in years! Don't you think I've grown up a little bit?"

"You have. In beauty as in years. But that won't stop you from poking around where you don't belong."

Emily leaned forward and kissed his cheek. "You are such a charmer! What woman could resist you if you put your mind to it?" She walked to the door. "I shall see you at the evening meal, cousin. Do dress your best."

William watched as she departed the room. He sighed softly, knowing she would try to get Grace to marry him. She would make matters worse and he would have to clean it up. Just like he did when they were children. He would have to warn Grace about how much Emily loved to meddle in his affairs. But he had to admit, he had missed Emily and it was good to see a family member who still loved him.

Grace sat in a chair as a servant girl braided her hair. She had taken a most welcome bath and had been given a fresh dress to wear. She was grateful for that. She was beginning to think the repugnant odor she was smelling was coming from her. As the servant girl, Anna, combed out her long hair and began to divide it into sections, Grace's mind wandered. To William. To the way he held her when they were coming into Bovey, to the warmth and safety she felt in his arms. But she had felt safe in Curtis's arms, too. Her imagination could be getting the best of her. Still, Curtis had never kissed her. At the memory of William's kiss, her lips tingled. She sucked in her lower lip. She replayed the kiss over in her mind. She had been shocked, of course, but then... Just as she realized what he was doing, just as she felt his lips on hers, felt the caress of his skin, he had pulled away. He had apologized and said he thought she was someone else. Someone else. She scowled and looked down at her hands entwined in her lap. Did he love someone else? She might have accepted that, except for one thing. Hadn't he said her name right before he kissed her?

Emily suddenly burst into the room, disrupting Grace's thoughts. She rushed over to her like a little whirlwind and looked her over. "What a lovely blue!" Emily exclaimed about the dress she wore. "It accents your eyes!"

"Thank you," Grace answered.

"Do her hair up," Emily told the servant girl, Anna. Anna bobbed her head and began to unbraid Grace's hair. "Are you comfortable here? Have your needs been met?"

"Oh yes!" Grace exclaimed. "Thank you for letting me stay. It's very kind of you."

Emily shrugged. "It's not my place to say. It's William's holding."

Grace nodded. "I shall thank him."

"What do you think of my cousin?"

Grace glanced at Emily. "Think of him?" she echoed.

"You are betrothed to him."

"Yes. Well... I think he is kind and strong and..."

"Handsome?" Emily encouraged.

Grace smiled at Emily's aid. She thought of William's strong jaw, his aquiline nose, and those eyes... Heat rose in her cheeks until she had to look away. "Yes. He is very handsome."

"He will make a fine husband, wouldn't you say?"

Guilt settled over Grace and a solemn mood descended. She had made him promise to help her escape the betrothal. "Yes. I would say that." He would make a fine husband. A very fine husband. For someone.

"How could any woman resist him?" Emily wondered.

"He's treated me with only respect." He had acted the part of a chivalrous knight. Better than Curtis ever had. Except for the kiss. And that kiss... That kiss made her feel alive and then disappointed. He had thought she was someone else. An idea came to her. Perhaps Emily would know who the 'other' was that William had spoken of. She looked at Emily. "I think he loves another."

"William?" Emily laughed but then tried to stifle it.

"There has been no one else. In all the years I have known him. No woman has caught his eye." She moved up to Grace and knelt before her, taking her hands into her own. "Only you."

"Me?" Grace echoed, shocked. She shook her head. "You are mistaken."

"You don't see it?" Emily asked. "The way he looks at you? It is as though the sun rises and sets with you."

Grace couldn't believe it. She stared at her dumbfounded. Had she missed it? Or was Emily seeing something that wasn't there? "It can't be true." Because somewhere inside her she wanted it to be true. And no man could ever find happiness with her. Not Curtis. Not her father. Not --

"It is. And you. How do you feel about him?"

Troubled by her questions, Grace stared into Emily's eyes. She didn't know how to answer. She'd never felt this way about anyone. Definitely not Curtis. He was more like a brother to her. She and Curtis were only friends. This was different. Every time she looked at William, or thought about his strong physique, his dazzling eyes, she felt a warmth blossom in her heart. A tenderness she had never felt for anyone. She was afraid to voice it. Afraid she would be wrong. Afraid he would reject her.

Emily patted her hand. "You'll have time, dearest." She rose and circled her, looking her over. "Perfect."

Grace stood and thanked Anna. "Shall we get William?"

"William doesn't dine in the Great Hall," Emily said.

"Why?" Grace wondered.

Emily frowned and sadness entered her eyes. "People can be cruel."

Grace nodded softly. Just like she was when she first met William. The immediate hatred and judgment she cast on him had come without thinking, without any effort to bring it forth. It was just there inside of her. She waited until Anna left the room before asking Emily, "Did he really do it? Did he really kill the archbishop?"

Emily cupped her cheek. "That is something you will have to ask him." She slowly dropped her hand in thought. "Perhaps he would dine with us if you asked him."

Grace stepped back, shaking her head vehemently. "I don't know what I would do if someone was cruel to him."

Emily clasped her hands tightly. "Ask him."

Emily had promised to meet her at the evening meal. She had said she needed to prepare a few things, but Grace had a suspicion Emily only wanted to give Grace time alone with William. It was something Grace would not argue with her about. She enjoyed the moments she and William spent alone together. She moved into the corridor and walked across the hallway to William's door. She lifted her hand to knock when she heard voices from inside.

"Why? Why did ya kill him? Was he a bad man?" It was a young boy's voice.

"The king ordered it," William answered.

There was silence for a long moment. Then the boy

said, "Me Mum says yer going ta burn in Hell."

"I am," William said softly, confidently.

His statement twisted Grace's heart.

"But ya did yer penance. Perhaps the Pope will forgive ya."

"There is no forgiveness for me. Let this be a lesson for you. God comes before king. In all things."

"Then how come ya killed the archbishop? Didn't ya know --?"

"I was greedy. I sought to gain the king's favor."

"Ya still got your lands! So the king must not be mad at ya!"

"A lot of good it will do me in Hell."

"Pray ta God. That's what I do when I did something bad. He always forgives me. He'll forgive ya too!"

"Thank you, Luke. I will try that. Maybe someday I will be forgiven."

Grace knocked softly on the door, hating to disturb the conversation. William opened it. Grace was unprepared for the sight that greeted her. He had cleaned up. He wore black boots and leggings that fit his muscular legs tightly. His white tunic was open at the neck, giving a glimpse of his strong chest. He wore his sword belted around his waist. His dark hair hung in waves to his shoulders. His blue eyes fixed on her with appreciation.

Realizing her mouth was open, she closed it and swallowed in a dry throat, all words lost. She couldn't remember what she was going to say. Her heart did a strange little flip in her chest.

He bowed slightly. "Lady Grace." His hand rested lightly on a boy's shoulder beside him.

Instinctively, Grace curtsied. "Sir William." Her knees almost weakened enough where she couldn't stand, but she managed to rise.

"Yer right," the boy said in awe. "She is beautiful."

Grace glanced at the boy, who was maybe seven summers in age, at the dark hair hanging in his eyes, and then back at William. Shock flooded through her. Had he said she was beautiful?

William took her hand and looked at the boy. "May I present the Lady Grace. This is Luke."

"Very nice to meet you, Luke."

Luke nodded, brushing his brown hair from his eyes. He looked back at William. "Remember, you promised."

William grinned and nodded agreement. "I remember. Go on, now. Make sure my dinner is ready."

Luke raced off down the hallway.

"I'm intrigued. What did you promise him?"

"That he could be my squire."

"Squire? He needs to be a page first!"

"Aye."

Grace looked at William. "You won't let him be your squire."

"I have no need of a squire." He opened the door to allow her entrance to his room. "Shouldn't you be in the Great Hall dining with Emily?"

"I've come to ask you to join us."

William's eyebrows rose in surprise. "Didn't she tell--" His words trailed off and he shook his head. Then he scowled. "It would be better if you ate with me in my room."

Grace folded her hands before her and looked

down thoughtfully for a long moment. When she looked up at him, warmth flooded through her cheeks. "Emily would be very disappointed."

"I do not dine in the Great Hall. You are most welcome to eat here with me."

"Why don't you eat in the Great Hall?" Grace wondered. "Is it because people can be cruel?"

William hesitated. "There are worse fates than being ridiculed." He looked into the room and then back at her. "Emily put you up to this, didn't she?"

"She suggested it."

William shook his head. "Grace... People... Knights don't always..." He took a deep breath. And then nodded reluctantly. "For you, m'lady."

William held Grace's hand as they entered the Great Hall for the evening meal. The room was not as big as the Great Hall in Willoughby Castle, but it still rose two stories above his head with beams criss-crossing high above. The clang of mugs and murmured talking filled the room. The tables lining the expanse were filled. William despised crowds. And this was no exception. He knew how they saw him, as a murderer, cursed, excommunicated. He didn't blame them. If it were just him, he wouldn't care. But Grace would see it now, see how flawed and horrible a man he was. She had asked him to accompany her. Was this what she wanted? Did she want to see him ridiculed? He glanced at her. She was stunning with her hair up, her neck flawless, her smooth skin magnificent. Her lips... How could he resist anything she requested?

The Great Hall was crowded, more so than usual, William guessed. They all wanted to see the man who killed Archbishop Becket. He was used to the stares. He was used to the hisses. He was used to the name calling. He could ignore them all. But he didn't want Grace subjected to them. He had informed steward Thomas as much, but he knew there was little the man could do about it.

He looked at Grace. She walked beside him up the main aisle, unaware of what the people around them were thinking. And maybe it was because of her they made it to the front table without incident. William took a seat beside Grace at the head table. He was glad she was there. She brought an unexpected light to his darkness, a joy to his worthless life. He could simply look at her all day. Her beauty outshone the bleakness. He was not worthy of her.

Emily sat at William's side, barely containing her delight. She leaned toward them. "I'm glad Lady Grace convinced you to come to the evening meal."

William grimaced. This was just the beginning of Emily's interference. William ignored her to cast his gaze over the crowd, assessing any threats. Many met his stare with open hostility. As dinner progressed, his attention became more and more focused on Grace. She talked and laughed with the man beside her, a young knight who reminded him of Curtis, charming him with her beauty. William was entranced by the way her lips moved, forming words. He remembered their softness beneath his, their pliancy, their gentle stroke. When the young man laughed and lay his hand over Grace's hand, rage ignited inside of William. He leaned toward them. "The lady is betrothed. You'd best remember that."

The young knight's eyes widened and he quickly removed his hand. Then he excused himself and left the room.

William's gaze followed him the entire way. Anger brewed inside of him, scorching reason, singeing the edges of his self-control.

"He was only telling me a story of when you were young," Grace said softly.

"He never knew me. It was all made up. You should learn to tell a lie from the truth." His words were harsh, and after he uttered them, he regretted them. He couldn't explain it. The anger and rage he thought he mastered had surfaced instantly. And over something that should not have bothered him. A simple touch. A possessive touch. Fury clawed up from that black cavern inside of him.

"Or maybe it was a story he heard and you are being irrational," Grace answered, her brows furrowing. She turned away from him and took a sip of her ale.

Yes. He was being irrational. That was it. Still, it took all of his will to banish the vehemence.

A knight at the far end of the table nearest them with a short beard suddenly rose violently, shoving his chair back with enough force that it crashed to the floor. "I shall not dine with a murderer." He spat on the floor.

William straightened at the insult. That was what he was used to and why he dined in his room, alone. How could he hold the knight to blame when what he proclaimed was the truth? It mattered not what the knight said, what any knight said. Only that he kept Grace safe.

Sporadic knights followed the short bearded knight's lead, heading down the aisle of the Great Hall.

Grace glanced at William.

He felt her eyes on him, but could not look at her for the embarrassment he felt. They were leaving because of him. Because of what he had done. Now she knew. He couldn't protect her from the scorn of others.

Suddenly, she stood and called out, "Halt you knights! What sort of impertinence is this? You will not dine at Sir William's table and yet you will work in his lands?"

"We work for his brother, Lord Ralph," one of the knights answered.

"And Sir William holds these lands for his brother. So, you answer to him as your lord."

"He murdered Archbishop Becket!" the knight with the short beard shouted. "I answer to no man who kills a man of the cloth!"

"Then you'd best find other work." A scattering of unease trickled through the hall like a gently swaying field of wheat. "Sir William is lord of these lands until his brother returns. Any man who doubts that or will not eat at his table has no place on his lands. Make your choice."

The knights glanced at one another; the whispering and low speaking grew louder in the hall.

William couldn't take his eyes from Grace. She was magnificent. Strong, commanding. It was what he should have done instead of hiding behind his past actions. Instead of cowering. He was a knight! But he had no wish for confrontation or to cross swords with another knight. So, he took the biting lash of their tongues in silence. Emily placed a hand on his arm. When he glanced at her, he saw surprise in her open mouth and raised eyebrows. She looked at William and a grin of enjoyment slowly stretched her lips and admiration shone in her eyes.

Finally, two of the knights returned to their seats. The short bearded knight left the room.

Grace lifted her chin and took her seat again.

William was stunned and humbled. She had defended him! He, a man who was not worthy of defending. She had done what he could not. She had faced the hypocritical knights and come out golden. He placed his hand over hers. "Thank you, Lady Grace."

She smiled demurely at him.

His heart pounded in his chest, his loins tightened. Lord, she was beautiful. And intelligent. How was he going to give her up?

CHAPTER FOURTEEN

When the meal was over, an energetic and a little too excited Emily led William and Grace down the corridor. "...roses and the cook has a small herb garden. She's teaching me how to plant. Because, as William knows, nothing I've planted has ever survived."

William didn't have the heart to tell her that when he was young, he found Ralph stomping on her newly planted growth. When he asked him why, Ralph said it was funny to see Emily so frustrated. He had never told her because it would break her heart. And he could never betray his brother's trust.

It was amazing the way the old memories came rushing back as they moved through the corridors. Ralph, Emily, his father, and mother. So many carefree recollections from his childhood. Chasing Emily down the hallway because she stole his sword. Walking down the hall with his father explaining the tallies. Hiding from Ralph behind the tapestry in a game of hide and seek.

He chanced a glance at Grace. She walked beside him quietly, looking up at the tapestries they past. Her clean hair was golden and styled up, allowing him a view of the line of her neck. Her skin was so smooth, so lovely. Kissable. The thought had entered his mind so quickly it startled him and he looked away...

...right into Emily's eyes. Her knowing gaze and slow grin caused him to scowl a warning at her. She was up to something, he was sure of it.

"The meal was lovely," Grace said.

William turned to her. Not as lovely as you, he thought.

"Lovely?" Emily snorted. "That impertinent knight! He should have been beheaded." She clasped Grace's hands. "But you handled it so well! Don't you think, William? Wasn't Grace spectacular?"

"Absolutely," William agreed.

"No," Grace protested. "He had no right. You pay him for his services. He pledged fealty to your brother. He has no right to speak to you thus."

A wave of guilt spread through William. She was right. Instead of taking a stand as she had, he hid in his room to avoid confrontation. He always told himself it was part of his penance, to endure the anger from others, to put up with their disdain without fighting back. Perhaps that attitude was wrong. He looked at Grace. Perhaps it was time for a change. "Either way. I thank you for what you did."

She looked at him, her eyes sparkling as they settled on his. "I could do no less."

His heart melted. God's blood, he was in trouble. How was he going to let her go without losing his heart? He couldn't stop looking at her. She was stunning. Her grin set desire flaring through his loins.

"Here it is," Emily said quietly, barely able to conceal the smile on her lips. She waited for a moment before opening the door. "Now, remember. This is only a small garden. Cook's and mine. But I'm very proud of it."

The door opened onto a starry sky. A trellis laced with roses led into a small area lined with herbs and vegetables. It was tucked away into a corner of the manor home that was basically useless for anything else. It was perfect.

Grace gasped. "It's beautiful."

Emily beamed with pride. She led the way through the small garden, which William noted was almost the exact size of the garden that was at the Mortain cottage. Emily pointed to a small corner. "Cook has let me plant here. These are mine."

"What have you planted?" Grace wondered.

"Onions." She pointed to a small line of growing plants. "See. There. And turnips."

Grace nodded. "They seem to be thriving."

Emily nodded, happily. "It makes me wonder if my earlier attempts weren't sabotaged." She glanced at William with narrowed eyes.

William held up his hands. "I can tell you truthfully that I never touched your plants."

Emily humphed and turned to gaze at her garden. "Oh! Goodness! I've forgotten. Cook asked for my help. I'm so sorry. I shall find you when I am done." She raced back through the door, leaving William and Grace staring after her.

They both watched the closing door for a long

moment in disbelief. William chuckled softly. "I must apologize, my lady. That was not very subtle."

"No," Grace agreed.

"Emily means well, but she is known to interfere in the affairs of others."

"I thought bringing us to this romantic setting and her quick departure seemed a little contrived."

"You are not insulted?"

"Not at all. I think it's delightful. Emily must love you very much. She is only doing what she thinks best for you." Grace sighed softly. "I wish I had a cousin like her."

"She would love to be your friend. I'm afraid we don't have many women in the Tracy family of Emily's age."

Silence settled around them, leaving them to look at the surrounding garden.

William's stare returned to Grace to find her gazing at him.

She laughed softly as if caught doing something she shouldn't. She glanced quickly away to the garden.

"I noticed you looking at the tapestries. What did you think of them?" William said.

"I love them. The colors are vibrant. Most tapestries that I have seen depict violent images of war. But the ones here show jousts and courtly love and falconry. They are beautiful."

William couldn't tear his gaze from her. He had never realized it, but she was right. Each tapestry lining the walls at the manor home were familiar to him, but he had never really looked at them. He should have noticed they showed no war or death or blood. It took Grace to point this out to him. Or did he simply see death and blood everywhere he looked?

Her blue eyes warmed and sparkled. A gentle breeze blew a lock of her golden hair across her cheek.

Except in Grace. He did not see despair and ruin. He only saw beauty and kindness in her. He lifted a hand to brush the strand aside, but froze. He was not worthy of a woman like Grace. She deserved someone who could give her serenity and happiness. He fisted his hand and lowered it.

Grace caught his fist in her small hands. "I was wrong about you, William. You are the most noble, honorable knight I have ever met."

William was shocked into silence. He shook his head to protest.

Grace cupped his cheek, stroking his skin with her thumb. "I want you to know that. I want you to believe that."

Again, William shook his head. "You don't know me."

"But I do. I know the man you are now. Your past doesn't matter to me."

Need and desire flamed through him. He knew he shouldn't believe her. But he wanted to. He knew he shouldn't kiss her. But he wanted to. He lowered his lips to hers, half expecting her to pull away, but hoping she wouldn't.

Grace lifted her lips to William.

He pulled her close and tight against his body, taking what she offered. God's blood! She was delicious and warm. He wasn't used to tenderness or softness. He wasn't used to be... being wanted. Her kiss was a breath of fresh air. She sighed softly against him and he plunged his tongue into her mouth, tasting her. Wanting her. All of her. Her body was soft against his. Her arms moved up his back, holding him. She was actually kissing him back!

He needed to save her. He pulled back from her, but kept her in his arms. He looked into her dreamy, half-closed eyes and arousal shot to life in him, filling his veins and his manhood. "You are tired, Lady Grace," he said softly. "I will see you to your room."

She blinked. And then blinked again as reality swept in around her. She stepped away from him, folding her hands before her. "Yes."

He guided her back toward the door, grateful for the gentle, cooling breeze. He opened the door.

Emily stood there, surprise in her wide eyes. As if she had been caught doing something she shouldn't. Then, a slow smile spread over her lips. "I was just coming back."

William narrowed his eyes. "I'm certain you were." She had been waiting here for them the entire time. Cook had not needed her help, he was certain. "Lady Grace is tired. I am showing her to her room."

Emily nodded. She seized Grace's hands. "Perhaps I could sleep in your room tonight! Just like sisters!"

William moaned to himself. He knew he should protest, but he knew it would do no good.

Emily pleaded with Grace to allow her to sleep in her room. Grace relented. How could she not? It was not her manor home. She was only a guest.

As Emily slept beside her, Grace stared at the moon through the shutters in her room. She was having difficulty falling asleep. Could she have been so wrong? Had her prayers been answered all along in William? He was honorable, noble, and so very handsome. His blue eyes weakened her knees. His kiss sent her world spinning, made her entire body come to life. She had to admit that she was falling in love with him.

Could the story of him murdering the archbishop be wrong? King Henry had not punished him, nor taken any of his lands away, so perhaps what William said was true. That the king had ordered the archbishop's killing. Or was she wrong and she was justifying what he did because she was starting to have feelings for him?

She turned over onto her back with a sigh. This line of thinking certainly wasn't going to get her any sleep. She saw a shadow move in her room. At first, she thought it was Anna, the servant that had been assigned to her. She glanced at Emily. But Emily hadn't moved. Grace sat up, trying to see into the room. Perhaps she had imagined it.

"Emily?" Grace whispered and reached out to shake her. Her fingers touched something wet. Confused, she stared at them for a moment. Then a shadow rose to life beside her, separating from the rest.

Instinctively, Grace pulled away from it. She slipped over the wetness near Emily and they both slid from the bed into a pile on the floor. Grace turned over in time to see the shadow on the bed. "Run, Emily!"

Someone was in her room! She was certain this time. She turned onto her hands and knees and crawled toward the door, calling, "William!" She managed to get her feet beneath her, but they caught in her nightdress and she fell onto her knee. She heard a whoosh over head. She tumbled forward and fell onto her back as the shadow flew over her head. The moonlight glinted on a metal blade whizzing past her.

She screamed.

CHAPTER FIFTEEN

William flung open the door just in time to hear Grace scream. He rushed into the room, the torchlight from the hallway washing into the room along with him. She was on the floor. He looked around, but could not see anyone else in the room. He rushed to Grace and saw red staining the side of her nightdress. He knew what the coloring was. He had seen it many times. His heart skipped a beat. Blood!

She pointed frantically at the door. "There! There!"

He dropped to his knees before her, grabbing her arms. "Are you all right?" he demanded, his gaze moving over her. He didn't give a damn who was here; he was frantic for her, terrified she was hurt. There was blood in her hair, on her clothing. "Are you hurt?"

"He's getting away!"

He shook her. "Grace! Are you hurt?"

She moved her head from side to side, her wild, round-eyed gaze focusing on him.

William glanced over his shoulder, but the

doorway was empty. He ran to the door and looked left and then right. Whoever did this was gone. He returned to Grace's side, afraid to leave her. He helped her stand. Concern marred her smooth brow and she looked at the floor near the bed.

"Emily," she whispered.

William followed her gaze. Dread spread through him as he saw a figure in white lying face down near the bed. He stepped by Grace, ordering, "Stay there." He hurried to the figure and knelt beside her. There was so much blood! It covered the floor and the bedding. He gently eased her onto her back.

Emily's limp body turned easily, falling into his lap. Her eyes were open, her lifeless gaze staring in accusation. Why didn't you protect me?

William's hands began to tremble. His gaze moved over her. A thin line across her throat oozed her life blood. Oh, Lord. Not Emily. Not Emily. Tears rose in his eyes. He had seen Death so many times. But he had never seen Him touch an innocent life. Except the archbishop. He almost dropped Emily at the thought. This was punishment. Punishment for his sin. He looked down at his blood stained hands. Everything he touched was damned. He was a fool to ever hope God would forgive him. He was cursed, doomed to the fires of Hell for all eternity. William clenched his teeth, gazing down at Emily. If he would never be forgiven, if there was no way to escape his future, then why honor his vow of never killing again? He wouldn't. He would find this assassin. He knew who it was. It was the man he had encountered at the Mortain cottage. He would find Peter and kill him.

William gritted his teeth. If he had killed him when

they were at the cottage, when he had the chance, none of this would have happened. He wouldn't have been able to hurt Emily. She would still be alive. But his vow had prevented him from shedding any more blood. Now, poor innocent Emily was gone because he didn't have the courage to kill again!

He brushed her blood-stained blonde hair from her forehead and carefully closed her eyes with trembling fingers. He held her for a long moment, unable or unwilling, to let her go. Finally, he slowly stood, unable to take his gaze from his cousin. Emily, his mind screamed. Little Emily. Rage swirled within him and he whirled...

Grace stood before him, tears staining her cheeks, her eyes red and swollen. She let out a small, shaky breath.

William hesitated. He was death and blood and destruction. How could he bring this to Grace?

"This is my fault," Grace whispered.

Shocked, William stepped forward. "No."

"The assassin was after me. Not Emily."

Horrified at her confession, William gathered her in his arms, comforting and taking comfort from her. He stroked her hair as the room came alive around them. Servants rushed in, steward Thomas entered. Someone screamed. And all he could do was hold Grace. She sobbed against his chest. William felt her agony. He had not been able to save Emily. How could he save Grace? But he would. He would do whatever he had to. She would not be harmed. He would not pass up the opportunity to kill the assassin. He would not miss that opportunity again.

Someone called his name, but his entire attention

was on Grace. William led her from the room to his room, housing her in the crook of his arm. Her face was buried into his chest. "You cannot blame yourself for this," he whispered sternly.

"If I had said no, that she couldn't sleep with me..."

He shook his head, peeling her away from him to look into her large teary blue eyes. He brushed back strands of golden hair from her cheeks. "No one says no to Emily. This is not your fault, Grace. The assassin did this. And he will die for it."

She bowed her head, putting her forehead against his chest. Her small hands were fists against his chest.

William didn't release her. He needed her as much as she needed him. He gently kissed the top of her head.

"My lord," a soft voice called from the doorway.

"It was the assassin," William replied with authority. "Have every man look for him. Detain anyone who does not belong. I can identify him."

"Aye, m'lord."

"And have Anna come to tend to Lady Grace."

Her fist clenched in his tunic as if preventing him from moving away from her.

"We must leave, Grace," William said quietly. "As soon as possible. I must get you back to your father. He can protect you."

Grace shook her head. "No. I don't want to. Not my father. He can't protect me."

"He will," William promised, his mind already formulating a plan to find the assassin.

"I don't want you to leave."

Her voice was so soft that at first William didn't think he heard her correctly. She was scared, that was all, he told himself. He rubbed her shoulders to calm her. "I'm not going anywhere."

William waited outside the closed door while Anna bathed Grace. The guard steward Thomas had assigned to the floor was dead. The assassin had snuck through the hallways, just outside William's door, and entered Grace's room. William thought she would be safe here for a day or two, at the least. He thought the assassin would head to Willoughby to search for her. Still... Something bothered him. Why was this assassin so intent on finishing the mission? Didn't he know Curtis was dead? There was no one to pay him.

It mattered not. Peter was a dead man. William would make sure of it. He would see Grace safely to her father. He looked down at the floor. The assassin had walked right past him. His hair fell forward and William lifted a hand to swipe it back. He paused. There was a smear of blood on his hand. Emily's blood. Emily. Anguish gripped him in a tight embrace. He dropped his hand, staring at the red stain. He had blood on his hands before. During the fighting in Jerusalem. But only once before had there been innocent blood on his hands. He didn't understand. He had promised never to shed blood again. And he had let the assassin live. And now, Emily was dead. What did God want from him? Why was He punishing him?

He looked down the hall toward the chapel. He wanted to pray. He wanted to ask for guidance. He wanted answers. He had done everything Pope Alexander had asked, and more. What did the Lord want of him? His fists clenched as his anger grew. Emily didn't deserve this. Was that what this was? The archbishop's innocent life for an innocent life that meant everything to him? His chest ached for his cousin. Never to hear her laughter again. Never to see the joy and mischief in her eyes. Tightness clenched his throat closed. Why couldn't God have taken him instead? Emily was just a child! Why take her? He had given everything, done everything asked of him. He had even made a vow never to shed blood again. But this was too much. It was a slap in the face. He had let the assassin live! And this was how God repaid him?!

The door opened and Anna stepped out. William straightened away from the wall.

Anna indicated the room solemnly with a tilt of her head.

William walked past her into the room. Grace sat on the edge of the bed. Her shoulders were slumped, her hands clasped. The blood had been washed away and her dress had been changed, but William could see she was still hurting. She lifted teary eyes to him. His heart broke. He rushed to her side and knelt before her. "I'm sorry, Grace," he whispered. Sorry about so much. Sorry for not being able to protect her. Sorry for not being the man she deserved.

She dropped to her knees before him, taking his hands into hers. "Don't. You've done enough."

"No. If I had, Emily would be alive. It was a mistake to come here."

Grace shook her head. "How could you have

known?"

"Because I told you. I thought to throw the assassin off our trail and come here instead of going to Willoughby Castle. But I did the same foolish thing Curtis did when he took you to his home. That was the first place they would look. I should have known this would be the place anyone tracking you would come."

She touched his cheek, stroking his skin. "You couldn't have known. This wasn't your fault."

He enjoyed her touch. It was warm and... bittersweet. She was a woman who didn't want him, and a woman he could never have. "We must leave come sun up."

She swallowed but didn't look at him. "And then?"

"I will hunt him." His voice sounded cold even to him. She snapped her gaze to meet his. Something passed in her eyes. Was it concern? Regret? Before he could decide, she looked down at their clasped hands. "You needn't worry, Grace. I promise I will not leave until you are safe."

"What of your safety?"

He was startled. She was the first to ever be concerned with his safety. "I am a knight." He stated it as fact. He didn't add the part about being cursed or regretting one moment in time for the rest of his life. "I am trained in battle. I will not fail in this."

"You are a man. You can be hurt or killed."

He released her hands slowly and straightened. "Who would mourn me? Perhaps my death would not be such a bad thing. I'm tired, Grace. I'm tired of the death that follows me like a shadow." He looked down at his hands where Emily's blood was like a scar, still smeared across his flesh. "I'm tired of the blood."

She put her hand on the side of his face, comfortingly. "I would mourn you."

He gazed into her eyes. They were brimming with compassion, forgiveness, and amazing strength. His stare dropped to her lips. They all but glistened, begging for his kiss. She would mourn him. A timeless spell descended on him. He was entranced by her soft hand on his face, her large eyes, her wet lips. He would remember this moment forever. And then she leaned toward him. He was so startled and wanted so desperately to kiss her that he couldn't move. He was frozen to the spot.

CHAPTER SIXTEEN

Grace pressed her lips to his. She was not experienced at kissing, but she knew she wanted to kiss William. His lips were like stone against hers, unmovable. Dismayed at her inexperience and inability to move him, she began to pull away. William suddenly reached around behind her and held her to him. His hand moved into her hair, holding her head against his.

The kiss was desperate and needing. It heated her entire body. He slanted his head, his lips coaxing hers to part. Gentle nibbles and strokes caused her to sigh softly. He plunged his tongue into her mouth, touching every part, every soft recess. He was hard and hot and strong and capable. Grace felt the world falling away around her.

Slowly, the heat and intoxication drained from his kiss. He placed a gentle kiss against her cheek and leaned his head against her shoulder. "Grace. Oh, Grace. You don't know what you're doing."

"I do," she insisted. "I know you love no one else.

There is no other woman. I know you told me there was to push me away from you. I know you were just trying to keep me safe. I know that you are as lonely as I am."

He pulled back to look into her eyes. Desperation shone from his blue eyes as his gaze swept her face. "What do you see in me that I cannot?"

She stroked his back, their bodies pressed tight against each other. Her lips still tingled from his kiss. They were still kneeling on the floor, wrapped in each other. He engulfed her completely in a blanket of security and safety and arousal. "William," she said softly and opened her mouth to continue.

"M'lord." A voice called from the doorway.

Both of them looked to find Steward Thomas standing in the doorway. William stood and helped Grace to her feet.

"I'm sorry to interrupt, but everything is ready."

"And Emily?" William asked.

Steward Thomas's head bowed. "She will be buried in the graveyard near the village church."

William walked up to him and lay a hand on his shoulder. "Thank you, Thomas."

Grace joined William at the door.

William took her hand and stepped into the corridor.

"The assassin, sir..." Thomas called, his voice laced with nervous fear.

"The assassin will follow us, I'm certain of it. You will not be bothered by him any longer."

Tingles of trepidation clawed up Grace's spine. William was leaving so the manor home and the village and everyone in it was safe. He was luring the assassin away, taking her away from his home so the assassin would follow them. Her hand tightened around his. She was surprised she agreed with him, and that she trusted him completely.

"What of this, m'lord?" Thomas asked.

Grace looked back into the room as did William. Thomas held the golden cross in his open palm, displaying it to William.

"I have no further need of it," William declared and led her down the hallway.

A shiver of disappointment and unease rolled through her at William's abandonment of the cross. Surely, the golden cross was just a material thing and meant nothing to him. She hoped it didn't. Because it had saved their lives once already.

They walked through the manor home and into the courtyard. Hellfire waited for them, saddled and fully loaded. William put his hands around her waist and lifted her into the saddle. Then, he mounted behind her, seizing the reins. He didn't look back at the manor home as he urged Hellfire through the streets. They moved at a quick pace, but as they neared the chapel William slowed his horse.

Grace glanced over her shoulder to see him gazing at the chapel door. In the night sky, the tall tower was a black shadow. She knew he took every chance he could to pray. She knew he needed to pray now, especially. "Do you want to stop?"

His jaw clenched and his eyes narrowed. "No." He spurred Hellfire.

Grace twisted in the saddle to watch as the chapel tower melted into the dark night sky, growing farther and farther away. A chill settled across her shoulders.

Something was different about William. There was something darker in his rejection of the cross. Maybe he was mourning his cousin. Yes. That must be it. Because Grace was afraid to think what else it might be.

The sun began to inch over the horizon, bathing the sky above them in a pinkish glow. With every movement of the horse, William felt Grace's soft body against his. It was distracting. He had tried to think only of the mission ahead of him, but every bump in the road, every lift of Hellfire's hooves pushed her bottom tighter against his manhood. It was likely to drive him crazy. He forced his mind to think of his cousin. Innocent Emily. He never should have brought Grace to Bovey. He should have known better. It didn't matter. He couldn't look back and think what if... He would make this right.

"I have to go home," Grace whispered, drawing William's gaze. "I have to see my father."

"Yes," William answered, but his mind was on other things. More blood. Broken vows. How he despised himself for being a fool. How could he ever have hoped to give up the sword? It was his destiny. Every time he swore it off, he was pulled back in. Either to defend himself or someone he loved. There would always be blood. No matter how much he prayed. There would be no more praying.

"Life is too short to be angry with someone you love," Grace said softly.

William tightened his hold on her. "Aye. That it

is." After Emily, after everything he had experienced, he knew how right she was. "Is that why you left? Because you were angry with your father?"

She took a long moment to answer. "I suppose that was part of the reason. I was angry with him because he betrothed me to you. I made assumptions about you like everyone else."

"Correct assumptions."

"No. I had the image of a monster, a devil. But you are nothing like that."

William remained silent. He was a monster. And he had to kill again to avenge Emily. He had to take another life.

"Why didn't you pray at the chapel?" she wondered.

William stiffened. When Grace shifted her gaze to look at him, he couldn't meet her stare. "He doesn't hear my prayers."

"I thought that, too. I used to pray for a knight to come and save me. To help me escape. When Curtis was killed, I thought God had abandoned me. But I was wrong. He hears all prayers."

William looked at her in disbelief. "Then why was Emily killed?"

She sighed softly. "I don't pretend to know His plans. But I believe that everything happens for a reason. You have to trust."

William shook his head. "I did trust. For years. I had faith. I sought His forgiveness. And this is how He repays me? By taking Emily?"

Grace placed a hand on his arm. "William --"

"No." He pulled his arm from her grip. Hellfire whinnied and tossed his head in response. "Enough is enough. I've done everything. Everything I was asked. And more."

She dropped her hand. "Did you really kill the archbishop?"

His fists tightened around the reins and Hellfire danced to the side before William righted him. "I'm as guilty as the rest of them."

"What happened?"

William thought back again to that fateful day. His jaw clenched tight. "I was a fool."

William had never intended to harm the archbishop. That was not the plan. The archbishop stood his ground, refusing to obey Reginald's command to come forth and allow himself to be taken to the king. And now Reginald was set on death. William knew he had to get the archbishop out of the cathedral before Reginald did something they would all regret. His friend was already far too angry to think rationally. William lurched forward, followed by the others, hoping to reach the archbishop first. He grabbed hold of the archbishop's white vestment, his hand fisting in the archbishop's garments, attempting to drag him from the altar.

But Reginald also grabbed hold of Archbishop Becket and pulled at him, trying to force him away from the altar.

The archbishop seized hold of one of the pillars as if it were a lover. He fought back, shoving Reginald from him. "Don't touch me, FitzUrse! You owe me fealty and obedience, you who foolishly follow your accomplices."

Reginald stumbled back away from Archbishop Becket before he righted himself. His face reddened in embarrassment and anger and he lifted his sword over his head, threateningly. "I don't owe fealty or obedience to you who are in opposition to the fealty I owe my lord king."

One of the monks rushed to the archbishop's aid, placing himself protectively before the archbishop to defend him from Reginald.

No, William thought. No. He fought harder to free the archbishop from the pillar, tugging at his arms.

A louder murmuring came from the group of monks Hugh was holding back with his brandished sword at the rear of the cathedral.

Richard seized the monk who was protecting Archbishop Becket and tried to disengage him from the archbishop, twisting his arms away from the archbishop.

William pulled at the archbishop's robes, trying to wrench him from the pillar he clung to.

Archbishop Becket inclined his head as if praying. Around him, chaos swirled in a vortex of confusion. "I commend my cause and that of the Church to God, to St. Mary and to the blessed martyr Denys."

With a cry of outrage and frustration, Reginald brought his sword down. The monk wrapped around the archbishop held up his arm to stop the blow. The sword hissed through the air, cutting the monk's raised arm and landed on the archbishop's head. The monk cried out, clutching his wounded arm and staggered away.

Blood flowed down the side of Archbishop Becket's face.

The scene froze. The monk recoiling in horror, blood staining the archbishop's face. William lifted his sword. If he could knock the archbishop out, he could yet save him. He brought the flat part of his sword down upon his head. It landed with a hollow thud.

Archbishop Becket still stood, but stumbled away from the pillar.

Reginald shoved the archbishop with a mighty push. The archbishop fell to his knees and elbows.

The archbishop was weakened. William reached for him.

They could now drag him from the cathedral and bring him to the king.

Richard lifted his sword high in the air as William moved forward, his hand outstretched to seize the archbishop. But it was already too late. Richard brought his weapon down with such force that it cut deeply into Archbishop Becket's head, slicing through his skull, moving through his head, to the stones below. The sword hit the stones with a loud clang and the metal blade split in two.

The archbishop collapsed. Blood flowed from his split head over the stones and down the steps.

Monks from the rear of the cathedral wailed and moaned.

William stared, horrified. His breath came in puffs. His heart raced. What had they done? His gaze lifted to the statue of Mary. She stared at him in silent condemnation. He should have stopped it.

Richard backed quickly away from the blood and dropped his broken sword.

The monk who had led them to the cathedral rushed toward them, taking the stairs to the altar. He placed his foot on the neck of the archbishop. Archbishop Becket did not move; he stared up with wide eyes. The monk kicked his brains across the floor and smeared the blood across the stones. "It is done, knights. We can now leave this place. He will not get up again."

William stared at the fallen archbishop. He lay at the top of the stone steps on his side, his hands still clasped as if in prayer, his white vestments stained with his blood. They had come to take him to the king. It wasn't supposed to be like this. He wasn't supposed to die!

William's cold eyes stared straight ahead. His lips thinned with anger. "I was wrong. We were so young.

So foolish. We sought to garner the king's favor. The plan was never to kill him. We wanted to arrest him, take him before the king." He shook his head. "But Archbishop Becket was obstinate and defiant. Righteous. We were all angry at Becket's audacity to refuse the king." He stared straight ahead. He could not take it back. It had been one moment in time. One moment he couldn't stop replaying over and over. One moment that followed him through his life with devastating consequences. Slowly, the anger drained from him. He could no longer capture that moment than he could the last breath, the last sunrise. "I just wanted him to let go of the pillar. I raised my sword. But he refused. I brought down my sword... I never meant to hurt him. I meant it as a threat. If I could have knocked him unconscious we could have just carried him back with us..."

Grace stroked his arm, encouragingly.

He had never told anyone the story before. He had kept it hidden inside, embarrassed by it. He felt compelled to continue. As if now that it was started, he couldn't stop it from escaping his lips.

"It got out of hand. I never meant..." He shook his head, his brow furrowing in anguish. "I think it was Richard who cut him next. I still just wanted to carry Becket back to the king. But we were angry. And it seems...maybe irrational. I hit Becket on the head with the flat part of my sword, hoping to knock him out. Hoping to save him. We could still arrest him. But it was not to be. The archbishop was struck once more and fell forward. Reginald cut him deep. And then Richard raised his sword and..."

Silence fell around them for a long moment. The

leaves of the trees rustled. The footsteps of the horse's soft clops could be heard.

"Do you think me a monster now?" William asked softly.

Grace wrapped one of his hands with both of hers. "A monster? Nay. I imagine that if the archbishop had gone with you, there might have been a different outcome. I imagine that if you had gone to talk to him alone, there might have been a different outcome. As it was, too many factors contributed to the death of the archbishop for it to have been any one person's fault."

William turned his head to her, his eyes wide in disbelief. "I killed him! There is no mistaking that."

"Nay. Yours was not the killing blow, was it?"

"I could have stopped it. I could have saved him..."

"Nay. You could not have stopped it." She squeezed his hand. "You could not have saved him."

William was silent, staring down at their entwined hands. He refused to believe this. He could have saved him. But he didn't. Perhaps, just perhaps, he could never have saved him.

Grace put her hand on the side of his face and he lifted his gaze to her. "I think there is only one thing to do now." She looked deeply into his eyes. "Forgive yourself. God has forgiven you already."

William scoffed. "How can you know that?"

"Because He sent you to me."

CHAPTER SEVENTEEN

William stared at her large trusting blue eyes. God did, indeed, send him to her. But was it some sort of mockery? She was so beautiful and forgiving and gracious. His heart ached. She was everything he could ever want. And he could never have her. She deserved so much more than he could offer.

He ripped his gaze from her. It wasn't forgiveness God was bestowing on him, but further punishment. His jaw clenched hard.

She lifted her hand to his cheek, her fingers trailing a soft touch over his hard jaw. "I love you, William," she whispered.

Startled, he snapped his gaze to hers. Disbelief held him as still as a stone statue as she pressed her warm soft lips to his. He shook his head. "You can't..." He breathed against her skin. She refused to be put off and continued the kiss. He couldn't deny her and didn't really want to try. With a groan, he relented and returned her kiss. She was a temptation he couldn't resist. He hardened instantly and shifted his position. When he pulled back to look down at her, even more confusion erupted in him. "I don't understand. After everything I told you."

"Because of it," she insisted. "All this time, they've made you out to be this horrible demon who killed the archbishop in cold blood."

"I did."

"No. You didn't. You tried to save him. The entire time. All you wanted to do was bring him before the king."

"That's all any of us wanted to do. In the beginning." He looked away from her. "It got out of hand."

"Oh, William," she sighed and framed his face with her hands, gently lifting his gaze to meet hers. "You are not the monster others see you as. You've treated me with the utmost courtesy and chivalry."

William shook his head firmly. "You can't love me. Think about it, Grace. There is no future, no family, for me. Any offspring I produce cannot be christened. I am excommunicated. Think about what you are saying. What that means."

"We'll make it work. If you are willing."

Her voice held all the excitement he should have been feeling. She said she loved him! And he knew he loved her. That was the problem. Because he loved her, he would never subject her to a marriage with him.

She straightened as realization crept through her. She clasped her hands and looked down. "Perhaps I am not what you want."

"What? No! I mean..." He had never allowed himself to hope. She was so beautiful. She was everything he wanted! But he had never dared to hope. Never thought it might be possible... He cupped her chin. "You are everything I want."

Those brilliant blue eyes grew wide with excitement. "Then you do...? You will...?"

"I love you, Grace. I suppose I have from the very first day I saw you."

With an excited squeal, she threw her arms around him. Startled, Hellfire rose up slightly on his hind feet, throwing Grace back into William.

William laughed as he hugged Grace. He couldn't remember the last time he had laughed. Perhaps Grace was right. Perhaps the Lord had forgiven him.

Suddenly, William heard a growing noise. The thunder of pounding. He reigned in Hellfire, keeping his arm around Grace, and looked toward the noise. Horses. Horses riding hard.

Grace heard the familiar sound of the pounding hooves a moment later. It wasn't one horse. It sounded like an army.

William turned Hellfire toward the forest.

Grace wasn't sure who was on the road, but she knew William was taking no chances. He dismounted behind some trees and helped Grace from the horse. Then, he quickly pulled out his sword. Grace's heart raced, pounding like the horse's hoofbeats stomping toward them.

"Stay hidden," he ordered her.

They watched the road through the branches and leaves of the trees. For a long moment no one appeared, even as the thunderous hoofbeats grew louder like an approaching storm. It was such an overwhelming sound. So loud. Grace reached out and clasped William's arm.

Then the army was there. And it was an army, an army of armored men on horseback racing by. It took a moment, but Grace spotted the heraldry the men wore on their tunics. It was a familiar symbol, a blue crossed pattern overlain with a black knight. She straightened. "My father," she said softly.

William lunged out, moving toward the road.

Grace reached for him, to stop him, to encourage him, she didn't know. Her fingers closed around air as he moved out of her reach and waved his arms, shouting to the men to stop.

Suddenly, her father's angry image rose before her, his scowling brow, his thin lips turned down in a pout. Would he forgive her? She had every intention of marrying William now. Could she convince her father it was all a misunderstanding? It didn't matter. There would be no further running for her. Determination filled her. She and William would face her father together. That thought gave her courage and conviction.

Men from the army gathered around William. He spoke to them and they turned to look at her.

Trepidation welled up inside of her under the barrage of their glares. Then she looked at William. He was not looking at her; he was speaking to a man on horseback. Without his calming presence near her, without his courage, fear churned in her stomach. Some of the guards dismounted and headed her way. Most of their faces were familiar and she should have felt comfort, but the thought of her angry father would not be banished from her mind. She was afraid of her father, she realized. Very afraid.

The guards asked her questions as they led her to the road, but she didn't hear them; she was looking at William. He stood a head over the rest of the men and was easy to find. He turned to look at her. Their eyes locked. There was something sad in his blue eyes. It wasn't comforting, nor strong.

He turned away then, heading into the forest.

Panic twisted her stomach. "No," she whispered more to herself than the guards. She attempted to follow William into the forest, but her father's men moved to block her path, attempting to herd her toward a horse. One man put his hands on her waist to help her mount, but she twisted and lurched away from him. "William!"

"M'lady," the guard said softly. He tried to take hold of her hand and prevent her from going into the forest.

She yanked her hand away from the man with such force she was propelled backward and fell onto her bottom. Booted feet trapped her like bars of a cage. She heard words, but in her anxiety didn't understand. A hand reached out for her. She followed it up.

William stood before her, his hand outstretched.

She reached for him, clasping his hand. He helped her to her feet. "She will ride with me," he announced and guided her into the forest toward Hellfire. "Courage, Grace," he whispered to her. "These are your men. They only mean to protect you."

They mean to take me away from you, she

thought, but didn't voice her concern.

The courtyard at Willoughby Castle was empty and dark as the soldiers followed William and Grace in. It was late and Grace was certain many villagers were abed. For the first time since she had runaway with Curtis, she had hope for the future. She couldn't wait to see her father and tell him of her love for William. She was certain he would be happy she had agreed to follow his order and marry William. And yet a nagging uncertainty, an unsettling anxiety, still gnawed at her.

William dismounted and helped her off of Hellfire. She smiled at him and he returned her happiness by lifting her hand to his lips. Grace kept his hand in hers and turned to the doorway. She stopped short. Her father stood silhouetted in the open door of the keep outlined by the dancing torchlight from the hallway. A demon. The thought erupted in Grace's mind and she took a step back, coming up against William's body.

William lay a comforting hand on her shoulder and it gave Grace courage. She was relieved he was with her. She took the first step toward her father. Her happiness faded beneath the rage she saw in his tight jaw and snarled lips.

William stopped her, catching her arm. He bowed slightly to her father. "She is safe, m'lord."

Her father's eyes did not move from her, locking on her like twin beacons of hate. Like a falcon eyeing its prey.

"Father --" she began.

"You defied me, girl," he ground out. "I would speak to you alone." He whirled and headed into the keep.

Grace glanced back at William. Dread slithered through her, snaking its way around her body, and for one beat of her heart, she couldn't move. William nodded reassurance to her. She didn't know what else to do. She followed her father inside the keep. Her footsteps echoed softly in the stone hall. Despite being inside the warm castle, a chill raced through her. How foolish she was for thinking her father would be happy to see her. Happy at all. She should have known he would be furious at her disobedience. He didn't know she and William had fallen in love. Perhaps when she told him... But something told her not to tell him.

She turned the corner in time to see him enter the farthest room. The judgment room. She followed after him, hurrying so as not to make him even angrier. The moment she entered the room he lashed out, striking her across the cheek with enough force to send her to the stone floor. Stunned, she stared up at his fury. His lips had curled back from his teeth, his eyes were wide. It transformed his entire face into that of an evil, hateful man.

"You willful whore," he snarled. "You leave with one man and come back with another. Did you bed them both? Like your mother?"

"Father," she whispered, shaking her head. Tears rose in her eyes. "I didn't --"

"Lies!" he shouted. "You disobeyed my order!"

She shook her head. "I will marry him! That's why

I returned. To follow your order. Father, please." She extended her hand. "I know what I did was wrong."

"Wrong?" The question came out as a roar.

"I love you."

"Love," he scoffed. He turned away from her, moving to the other side of the room, near the hearth. The light of the dying fire cast him in a red glow. He suddenly began coughing. It started with a small gasp and sputter, but quickly turned into a fit of thick rumbles.

She sat up, confused at her father's rage, afraid he would strike her again. Yet, he was her father, and no matter what, she knew she had to help him. When his coughing stopped, she whispered, "I will do as you command, Father."

"Do as I command?" he repeated with a small, strangled laugh, wiping his mouth with the sleeve of his black jupon.

"I don't understand, Father. Isn't that what you want? My marriage to William?"

"I don't care who you marry, as long as you are miserable. I only consented to the marriage because I thought you could never love a man like him, a cursed man. A monster. A killer."

She stood to her feet, her knees trembling. He had wanted her to marry William so she was unhappy. "Why? What have I done to displease you?"

"Displease me?" He stepped from the shadows, his face twisted and loveless. "You were born!"

"But... We were happy when Mother was alive."

"Because I didn't know. I didn't know you were not mine."

She stepped back, reeling. No words escaped her

open lips.

"Your mother told me when she was sick. She told me she loved another. She told me she was unfaithful. She told me she had fucked another man!" He swiped at a small chair beside the judgment chair, launching it across the room. It smashed into the wall, splintering. "She told me all of it to cleanse her soul, she said." He waved his hand. "Or some such rubbage. I was furious." He looked down at his hands and clenched them into fists. "So furious. I killed the little slut. I killed my wife. I strangled her."

Stunned, horrified, Grace couldn't move. He had killed her mother! The image of her mother laying half off and half on the bed came to her mind. She had been sick and Grace had believed she had simply passed. She hadn't seen the marks around her neck. Her fingers moved to cover her mouth. He had killed her!

"But I will have the last say. I will make sure nothing of her loins, no bastard born slut, will be happy. That was why I arranged your marriage to that cursed degraded soul. You would be as cursed as him. Destined for hell." He shook his head. "But he didn't come. And I was running out of time."

Grace stepped toward the door. He was mad. He was out of his mind. She had to get out of that room, away from him. Her stomach tightened and churned in fear. He had killed her mother.

"I had to act quickly. So very quickly." He ran his hand over the wooden arm of the judgment chair, caressing it. But his gaze never left her. "Plotting and scheming. You think I am a fool. Your mother did. Is that what you think?"

"Father --" she whispered, weakly.

"I'm not your father!" he howled.

She could only stare in horror as he continued his rant.

"I sought out a knight who wanted to better his position. A knight more concerned with coin. A young knight. A knight who didn't care about chivalry. Your friend. Together, we hatched a plan. He would take you away. Far away. Saying he would save you. I even gave him more coin to take you away."

Pain twisted Grace's chest at his story. "Curtis," she said softly.

"Yes. Yes. But it wasn't enough for me. I couldn't stand the thought of you somewhere enjoying the sunshine and laughing. Maybe finding a fat little baker boy to settle down with." He ground his teeth.

Grace felt her world spinning. A plot. It was all a plot. Curtis was her friend! Someone she trusted. But it had been a plan hatched with her father. Between the two of them. She glanced at the door as she slowly inched her way toward it; she was almost there. She knew she had to escape. She had to get to William. "I don't understand."

"Yes, it's difficult for you to follow." His voice was thick with mockery. "Once I realized my mistake in letting you escape with a friend, I knew what I had to do. I could not stand the thought of you walking the same path I might walk. Of breathing the same air I would breathe. There really was only one choice. I was a fool not to do it earlier."

Tears rose in her eyes. How could he hate her so much?

Her father started laughing, but the coughing returned, doubling him over with spasms. He had to sit in the judgment chair to calm his wracking sputters. He announced through the coughs with glee, "I hired someone to kill you."

CHAPTER EIGHTEEN

Stunned and horrified, Grace couldn't move. Emily had died because of her father! It hadn't been Curtis. Curtis had been loyal to her.

Her father slumped over in the chair, and for a moment, Grace thought he might be dead. She glanced at the door, every instinct telling her to flee. He tried to kill you! He killed your mother!

"I would have done it myself," he whispered, "but the only joy in my life is seeing you hurt. It is the only way to get back at your mother. You were her only love. She protected you. She gave you everything you wanted. Now. It is my turn." He rose out of the chair like a demon, like Death.

Grace lunged for the door. She wrapped her hand around the handle.

His hand knotted in her hair. "Where are you going? I didn't give you leave to exit." He yanked her back into the room.

She rolled across the floor, coming to a halt before the chair.

Her father opened the door. "I shall be back to tend you later."

Grace pushed herself up on her arms. "Where are you going?"

"You and Sir William looked far too comfortable together. I must tend to him first. Be patient."

"No," the sound escaped her throat and she pushed herself up from the floor and raced across the room. Her father closed the door before she could reach it. She grabbed the handle desperately, but she was too late. The lock slid into place with a resounding click.

William waited in the courtyard for a long while. He stared at the doorway, looking for Grace. He looked at the stars, at the walkways where the guards were stationed at their posts. Eventually, his gaze was drawn to the doorway again. Something was amiss. He could feel it in his bones. Enough time had past for Grace to talk with her father and explain their situation.

He walked into the keep. His senses were heightened. He had to find Grace. There was an urgency to his mission. Her father didn't know about the assassin.

The hallway was barren as he looked first one way and then the next. Noises came from the courtyard. Someone shouted to another person. A horse whinnied. He started to move down the hallway when he heard a door open. William whirled. Lord Alan walked toward him, a grumbling cough causing him to cover his mouth as he moved. When Lord Alan saw him, he began to move toward William with resolve.

William waited for him. "M'lord," he greeted with a slight bow. "I've returned your daughter."

He nodded. "Yes, you did," he agreed.

Was that disappointment in his tone? William scowled. "Grace and I wish to fulfill your wish and be married."

"I'm afraid after speaking with her, she told me she wanted nothing to do with you."

William took a quick inhale of utter astonishment.

"I'm sure she confessed her love to you, as she did to Sir Curtis. She uses her love and her body as a means to get what she wants. And she wanted to return home. That was all."

That was not the truth. She wasn't like that. William didn't believe what Lord Alan said, but why would the man lie to him? "What of your vow to my father?"

"Yes. Well, that is difficult for me. But I cannot force my daughter into a marriage she does not want."

Prickles danced along William's neck. That exactly what he was doing before. He was forcing Grace to marry him. William was certain the man was lying to him. "Where is Grace? I would like to speak with her."

"She said she didn't want to see you again."

The words set William's jaw on edge. If he had harmed her...

"I know this must come as a blow to you. After I agreed and all. But you must understand..."

William stood, rooted to the ground. What could he do? His mind raced. He couldn't leave Grace, and yet he saw no alternative. He nodded. "I have traveled a great distance, Lord Alan," he said. "And returned your daughter to you. Perchance I might ask a cup of ale and a warm meal before I depart?"

Lord Alan nodded. Suddenly, a cough bubbled from his throat. He caught it with his fisted hand and one cough turned into two and then more until he was bent over in a fit.

William put his hand on Lord Alan's shoulder. "Do you need help? Should I send for a physician?"

Lord Alan shook his head. "I shall be all right." He removed a piece of cloth from his sleeve. The white fabric was stained with splotches of smeared blood.

William knew he would not be all right. It was only a matter of time. He had seen it before. The man was dying. William withdrew his hand from Lord Alan's shoulder.

Lord Alan straightened, dabbing at his lips with the material. "Yes. Yes. You shall have your meal. Go into the Great Hall. I shall have it brought to you immediately."

William turned to go when something caught his eye. The material Lord Alan used to wipe his mouth was embroidered with a black cat in the center. He had seen that black cat before. But where? He nodded. "Thank you, Lord Alan."

Lord Alan's shoulder's drooped. "I will be unable to join you. For at the moment, I am fatigued."

William nodded and watched the man move past him toward the stairs and the upper chambers. That black cat grated his nerves. He had seen it before. He could see it clear as day in his minds' eye. But he couldn't place it. That damned cat, William thought. He looked at Lord Alan's retreating back again before heading into the Great Hall.

Grace shook the door again, but no one came to unlock it. She glanced around the room. It was dark except for the dying fire in the hearth behind the judgment chair. She leaned against the door, staring at the fire. He had killed her mother! Sadness engulfed her. How could he have done that? How could he have killed the woman he professed to love? Because he had never loved her mother. Just as he had never loved her. That would explain why he hated her so much. Why he wanted her to be miserable.

But none of it mattered now. She had to find William.

William. She wondered what her father was telling William, what ugly words he was using to hurt him. William had endured enough. He didn't need more lies and more pain.

She stepped away from the door and began to walk around the room, looking for some way out. There had to be something she could use to escape.

He wasn't her father. That explained the hatred she saw when she looked in his eyes, the disgust that curled his lips when he saw her. But it didn't really. He had raised her as his own. She was still his daughter.

Suddenly, she heard the bolt sliding. Someone was

unlocking the door. Anticipation surged within her. Was it William? Had he found her? But then she realized how unlikely that would be. It must be her father coming back to hurl insults and lies.

The door swung open. Desperation and dread left her breathless as fear tightened within her.

The assassin stood in the doorway.

CHAPTER NINETEEN

Grace backed away from the door toward the hearth.

The assassin stepped into the room, closing the door behind him.

Her heart pounded. He was the man she had seen in the woods at Curtis's cottage. She recognized his thick dark beard. "It was you. You killed Emily," she whispered.

He said nothing as he moved toward her. Slowly, almost as if enjoying the moment, he produced a dagger from his belt. The silver blade shone in the firelight.

Firelight. Grace glanced down at the dying fire, spotting a log that had been partially burned.

"You are hard to kill," the man said softly.

She grabbed the log with both hands, burning one of her hands in the process, and yanked the wood out of the hearth. Embers sprayed about the room as she quickly raised the log up, holding it before her.

The assassin covered his face as tiny barbs of flame

shot toward him.

Grace saw her chance. She raced past the assassin and was almost to the door when it opened. Thinking her father was returning, she lifted the log to hit him. All her thoughts centered on escape. Escaping her father. Escaping the assassin. Escaping. She froze as the man entered. Even though his face was shadowed in blackness, she would know him anywhere. "William." She dropped the smoking log and launched herself into his arms.

He caught her easily, his gaze locked on the assassin. He eased her to the side so he could pull out his sword.

Grace looked up at him. She had never been so happy to see anyone in her life.

His entire focus was on the assassin near the hearth. "Are you hurt?" he asked Grace, keeping his gaze on the deadly killer before him.

"No," Grace answered.

William stood before her like a tower of death. His sword shone in the firelight. "I remembered where I saw that cat," he whispered.

The assassin pulled on a thin leather cord that hung around his neck, drawing forth a pendant that dangled from the end of the cord. He held the pendant before the fire. It cast a black shadow of a cat on the wall. "The black cats are deadly and lethal. Highly trained."

"Highly expendable," William snarled.

The assassin tucked the pendant back into his tunic.

"My father hired him," Grace said softly. "It wasn't Curtis."

"Your father is responsible for Emily's death?" William asked with dangerous surprise. He gritted his teeth.

"You'll never prove that," the man near the fire vowed.

William raised his sword. "I won't have to."

Grace stepped back. She moved to the door and quietly closed it, sealing the three of them in the room. She didn't want anyone interfering, least of all her father.

"Not very noble of you, eh William?" the assassin said, displaying his dagger, and indicating William's sword with a jerk of his chin.

"You killed an innocent woman," William accused. "My cousin."

"Unfortunate. She wasn't the woman I was after."

Anger pulsed through William. He had killed Emily as a mistake. Taken her life because he had meant to kill Grace. He had no intention of letting him near her. And he would avenge Emily. There would be no mercy for this killer. William took a step toward him. Evil came in many forms.

The assassin threw the dagger at him and drew his sword.

William knocked the dagger aside with his sword only seconds before the assassin attacked. William deflected the first blow and answered with his own swipe. The clangs rang out, echoing through the air. William refused to circle or give him ground. He would not let him get a foot closer to Grace, not an inch. It took all of his skill to keep the man back. He was an excellent fighter. The swords blazed through the air, arcing and clashing again and again.

He was good. But he wasn't a trained knight. He kept to the shadows, attacking his prey in the dark. Faced with a sword, head to head, the assassin was not skilled enough. It took William only moments to find a weak spot in his style and he took advantage, thrusting. His mighty movement drove his weapon forward, past the assassin's sharp sword, into his armorless stomach. Surprise washed over Peter's face.

William had seen death many times before. From an innocent archbishop to soldiers in battle to his defenseless cousin. This was, truly, the only satisfying death. He thrust his sword deeper into the man's stomach. "For Emily," he whispered. Suddenly, he felt a burning sensation in his arm and looked down. The assassin had pricked him with a small dagger near his elbow. William knocked it aside. It didn't matter. He had avenged Emily. He had saved Grace.

A small smile turned up the corner of the man's bearded lips before he slumped forward. William pushed him backward, off of his sword. He stood over him, staring down at the corpse. The image of Emily's dead body come to his mind. It didn't bring her back. He would never see her smiling face again, hear her teasing words. But this man would never be able to kill again. And that was some sort of satisfaction.

William turned to Grace. She stood near the door, watching.

She lurched forward into his arms. "Are you all right?"

He caught her, holding her. Relief swept through him. No one would try to hurt Grace again. She was safe. He bent his head and rested his cheek on her golden hair. It was over.

There came an urgent knock on the door. "M'lady?"

William stepped away from Grace. He held up a hand to her, signaling her to wait, and eased the door open to find a servant girl. Her brow was furrowed in concern. William opened the door further until the servant saw Grace. She curtseyed. "Pardons, m'lady. But it's your father. He has collapsed."

Grace moved forward. "Where?"

The servant girl led the way down the corridor.

William grabbed Grace's arm. "Grace! We should leave. Your father tried to have you killed."

"I know," she answered. "But he is sick. He is dying." She turned and followed the servant down the hallway.

William took a step after her. The room tilted to the side. Stunned, he stood as the room around him moved. He glanced back at the assassin on the floor. Was this some sort of trick? Then he looked at his arm where the assassin had stuck him. Dread filled him. He raced after Grace. The cool air of the hallway cleared his head momentarily. He saw her running into a stairwell and called to her, but she didn't stop. He continued after her. The hallway darkened around him, hedging in from the borders, but he continued on. He had to reach her. He entered the curved stairwell and the entire walkway tipped. The steps seemed to grow and twist, rising before him like a mountain. He took one step and then another. Every step was becoming difficult. This can't be happening, he thought. Not now. Not when he had won the woman he loved. Not when he had avenged Emily. But he knew that was exactly why this was happening. He broke his vow never to kill again. He had doubted the Lord above. And he was being punished.

He reached the top floor and saw Grace through a long tunnel in the far distance as she entered a room at the end of the hall. He stumbled forward, sweating profusely now. He leaned on the wall, looking down the corridor at the door. If he could only make it there. Only see her one more time. One more time. The fires that waited for him would mean nothing next to her beauty and her love. If only...

He tried to take another step, but stumbled and fell to one knee.

It took all of his strength to rise. His entire body shook. He looked at the cut on his arm. The red slice in his skin looked innocent enough. But William knew it wasn't.

He looked up again at the door. The hallway seemed to lengthen and waver before his eyes.

Someone said something. He looked over his shoulder and saw the servant girl who had knocked on the door. She looked at him with fear and apprehension. "Help me reach Grace," he said softly.

She replied but her voice was garbled and unintelligible.

He reached out to grab her arm and she pulled away. He toppled to the floor like a felled tree. He wasn't going to make it. Darkness ate away at the borders of his sight. He wasn't going to make it. The darkness was tinged with the fires of Hell.

CHAPTER TWENTY

Grace entered the room. Her concern for her father overrode all other emotions. She knew no fear. She knew no hate. The room was silent and dark. She stepped around the massive four-post bed and spotted him on the floor. Father! She raced up to him, falling to her knees at his side. The image of her mother came to her mind. Her father lay much the same as her mother, on his side, unmoving. "Father," she whispered. When he groaned, she eased him over onto his back.

He coughed and droplets of red sprayed across her dress. He tried to push her hands away, but he was so weak he was barely able to lift them from his sides. He shook his head, still fighting her.

As Grace stared down at him, she saw him as if for the first time. Powerless. Loveless. Afraid and alone. "It's all right, Father," she said softly and stroked his forehead to soothe him. "It's all right."

He shook his head angrily, but there were tears in his eyes.

"I'm here," she said and gently kissed the top of his head.

He choked and wheezed, unable to talk.

She gently lifted his head and placed it in her lap. She stroked his hair, trying to calm him. "It doesn't matter," she whispered. "Mother made a mistake. And I was born of that mistake. But I have always been your daughter." His shoulders shook and she wasn't sure if he was sobbing or if he was groaning angrily.

Suddenly, a scream rent the air. She looked toward the sound. She eased her father's head to the floor and raced to the doorway. The servant woman stopped before her and clasped Grace's hands. She glanced over her shoulder, down the hallway. Grace stepped from the room to find William on the floor. She looked at the servant. "Get someone to tend my father." Her heart twisted painfully in her chest and she rushed to William, dropping to her knees at his side. "William," she called.

His eyes opened to mere twin slits. His lips moved. She bent closer. "I can't hear you, love."

"Poison," he repeated.

Horrified, Grace looked at the terrified servant who hadn't moved from the doorway and commanded, "Get the herbalist. Now! Go!" The woman raced away. No, no, no. Her mind repeated over and over. They can't have made it all this way for nothing. "William," she said, wiping his brow, his cheeks. He looked so pale. His usually tanned skin was almost white. She couldn't stop touching him, didn't want to stop touching him. "You saved me." Her throat closed around her words; her eyes filled with tears. This can't be happening. She kissed his lips, his cheeks. "I love you."

He lifted a hand to cup her cheek. "You saved me."

Startled, she looked into his eyes. There was a grin on his lips, a twinkle in his blue eyes. She hugged him, sobbing. "No," she gasped. She wouldn't lose him. She couldn't lose him. He was her strength. He was her safety. He was her love. "I'm so sorry, William. I'm so sorry." She had been wrong about him. She had misjudged him in all ways possible.

"Don't," he grumbled. "Not sorry."

She pressed her fingers to his lips. "Save your strength." She swiped at her eyes, trying to clear the tears blocking her view of him. "The herbalist will be here any moment."

He caught her hand. "Grace."

She saw the agony in his blue eyes, in the fire behind his orbs. "Don't leave me," she begged.

He closed his eyes.

There is a reason for everything, she told herself as the tears dripped from her eyes. But she couldn't figure out what the reason behind taking William from her was.

Grace stayed with William through the night. The herbalist told her there was not much hope. He advised calling a priest. Grace refused and closed the door. She knelt at his side, praying. Praying for his soul, praying for his recovery, praying for forgiveness. She had just found him, just realized she loved him. Why? She picked up his hand and kissed it. It was limp and hot in her hold. He had always been so confident, so strong.

Why save her just to take him away? Why take the man she loved? She remained on her knees, holding his hand. Begging the Lord not to take him.

Could this be William's punishment for losing faith? No. "Please," she whispered. "Please just give him another chance to redeem himself."

Darkness circled about her head, and she ran. Ran from something. Or to something, she didn't know. She only knew she had to reach it. Not it. Him. She saw William lying on the ground. She knelt beside him, but there was something heavy on her head. She tried to brush it away, but it refused to move and she couldn't see what it was. She didn't care. William was all that was important. She reached out to him, but he was suddenly swallowed by the darkness.

"No!" Grace sat up straight. She looked around the room in disorientation. It took her a moment to realize she was in her old room at Willoughby Castle...

...and that William's eyes were open. She gasped and moved to the bed. "William?" She touched his forehead. It wasn't warm. It was sweaty and moist, but there was no fever. Her gaze moved over his handsome face, from his strong nose to his sensual lips. She brushed a kiss against them.

"Thirsty," he whispered.

She jumped up and moved to the table to pour him a mug of ale. She returned, cradled his head in the crook of her arm and pressed the mug to his lips. He took a deep drink. She placed the mug on the table and knelt beside the bed, unable to stop touching him, his face, his hands, his chest. "How do you feel?"

"Weak."

"I guess there will be no fighting off assassins for you."

He chuckled softly. "Not today."

"Oh, William. They said you wouldn't make it. They said to call a priest. They said there was no hope."

William's lips twitched and he nodded. "It wouldn't be the first time." He moved to sit up.

She gently pushed him down. "Rest. Please." She had to get his mind off of getting out of bed. "You'll need your strength for our wedding night."

He scowled. "Your father agreed?"

She lifted her eyebrows and averted her gaze. "He can't exactly disagree. His illness has made him too weak to move, too weak to even speak."

"Lady Grace," he said softly, "are you thinking of defying your father?"

"Not at all. He said to marry you and I shall." She lifted her chin. "I shall be the perfect daughter and marry the man my father ordered me to marry."

William smiled.

Grace felt her heart leap; she could barely control her answering grin. He was better. William was going to live!

"Yes," he agreed. "Perfect."

She shook her head. "I don't understand. The herbalist said there was no hope. That it was likely you wouldn't make it through the night."

He shifted his weight and turned his head to the side, away from her. "Well, if that is what you want."

She grabbed his shoulder and cupped his chin, easing his gaze back to her. "There is nothing I want less."

"It was nightshade, wasn't it?"

"Nightshade?" she echoed.

"The poison."

She scowled, hating the word. Poison. Nightshade. "Yes. I believe the herbalist mentioned something like that."

"When I was in Jerusalem, there was an attempt on my life. They used nightshade. The same thing was said then. They had almost begun digging my grave."

Alarmed, Grace clung to his hand. "You recovered."

"Aye. As I did this time. I must have some sort of resistance to it. I suppose I should be grateful it was nightshade."

"Perhaps someone was looking out for you."

William reached for her. "My future wife."

As his arms wrapped around her, pulling her against him, she knew he had been forgiven. And he was being given a second chance. She would make certain he took advantage of it.

CHAPTER TWENTY ONE

William watched with his arms crossed over his chest as the last stone was placed at the top of the tower of the newly named St. Peter, St. Paul, and St. Thomas in Bovey. It was not enough penance, he knew. Not in the least, but it was a start. He was pleased the new church was close to being finished.

Father John emerged from the church door, shaking dust from his thin white hair. He brushed at his shoulders and more dust clouded off of him. He had been the only priest willing to marry him and Grace. Grace had made Father John promise he would not tell anyone he had married them. She didn't want him to be excommunicated, and neither did William. His wife was very smart. It had been a small ceremony, held under the night stars in the clearing just south of Bovey.

It was perfect. He could not have asked for more.

Father John hobbled over to him. "Those incompetent..." His voice lowered to a mumble.

William smiled. "Careful, father. A man of the

cloth has to set a good example for his people."

"And how would you know, boy?" Father John grumbled. "You stand out here all day with that cursed grin on yer lips. As if you have it all figured out! I would like you to figure out how to get these masons to speed up construction!"

"Perfection cannot be rushed."

"Perfection? I can build an entire cathedral in the time it's taken them to build this one church."

"They are taking their time because it amuses them to see you so ruffled."

Father John sputtered, and his wrinkled face turned red.

William laughed.

"William!" a feminine voice called.

He turned to see his wife riding up on her new white mare; two mounted men rode behind her. She always took his breath away. Her beautiful blonde hair waved out behind her, a blush from the wind touched her cheeks. She was so lovely and again, he thanked the Lord for her. She dismounted by herself, throwing her leg over the side and sliding to the ground. "William. Are you giving Father John a difficult time?" She set a calming hand on Father John's arm. "There there, father. Pay him no heed."

"I've tried, m'lady, truly I have. But this racket would drive me from my own church!"

William locked gazes with Grace. A sly grin touched the corners of her lips.

Without removing her gentle touch from Father John's arm, she said, "William, we have visitors."

William looked back at the men on horseback as they dismounted. Although their appearance was gruff and older, he recognized them immediately. He came forward. "Hugh! Richard!"

Hugh reached him first, wrapping him in a tight embrace. "It's been too long," Hugh greeted before giving him up to Richard.

Richard held his arm out for the customary warrior greeting.

William brushed aside his hand and grasped him tightly. They were brothers. And there was no other way to greet a brother. These were the men he had gone through hell with. Literally, although now each had their own personal hell to endure. "You look weary," William said, slapping Richard on the shoulder.

"When we heard about Emily, we rode as quickly as we could," Richard said.

William nodded and glanced toward the cemetery where his cousin was laid to rest.

"I'm sorry," Hugh said sincerely.

"Aye," Richard agreed. "She was a good child."

William nodded again. "I'll miss her." Grace came up beside him, placing her comforting arms about his waist. He lifted his arm to drape it around her shoulders and draw her closer. He exchanged a loving glance with her. "Have you met Lady Grace? My wife."

Hugh's mouth dropped open. "Your wife?"

Richard's eyebrows shot up as he looked Grace over appreciatively.

"How? I mean... Does she know?"

"She knows," Grace said, gazing at William with appreciation. She lifted on her toes to press a kiss to his cheek.

William looked down at her. How had he gotten so lucky? Sometimes, anguish rose in him as he held her in his arms late at night. He didn't deserve her. He was amazed that she looked at him with such tender devotion. And then he grew fearful. What if he awoke and discovered it all a dream?

"How did you marry? What priest would risk the Pope's wrath?" Hugh asked.

William grinned. "A friend. A very good friend. We are keeping this quiet. Not because I don't want to yell to the top of the mountains, but because I will have no one else hurt because of me."

Hugh and Richard nodded in understanding.

"Congratulations," Hugh said sincerely.

"You are one lucky bastard!" Richard added with a laugh.

"Come, m'lords," Grace called. "You look as if you've ridden nay on a month. We have warm rooms and good food for you."

"Finally!" Richard called. He followed her toward the manor.

Hugh hung back as Father John walked toward the church, mumbling about fallen stones. "Any word about Reginald?" he asked softly.

William shook his head. "I haven't heard from him since Jerusalem."

Hugh nodded. "It's good to see a smile on your face."

"It's good to have a reason to smile."

"Come m'lord!" Grace called to William. "It is time to relax with your friends."

Hugh chuckled as he followed William to Grace's side. "You've found your redemption."

Shocked, William stopped to look at him. "I suppose I have." He hurried after Grace, who was waiting for him, and took her into his arms, holding her tight against him. "More correctly," he told Hugh while gazing into those large blue eyes that had captured his heart. "I've found my Grace."

Dear Readers -

This novel is based on fact; there were indeed four knights who killed Archbishop Thomas Becket. William de Tracy was one of these knights. Not much is known about them after they were excommunicated and went to fight in Jerusalem as penance. I hope that each of them were truly sorry for the horrible act they committed. In my story, William is forgiven and he does finally find peace.

The next book in the Assassin Knights series is A Knight With Hope. Please subscribe to my website - www.laurel-odonnell.com - so you won't miss the upcoming release.

Thank you for reading William and Grace's story!

COMING SOON!

A KNIGHT WITH HOPE

ABOUT THE AUTHOR

Bestselling author, **Laurel O'Donnell**, has won numerous awards for her works, including the Holt Medallion for **A Knight of Honor**, the Happily Ever After contest for **Angel's Assassin**, and the Indiana Golden Opportunity contest for **Immortal Death**. **The Angel and the Prince** was nominated by the Romance Writers of America for their prestigious Golden Heart award. O'Donnell lives in Illinois with her cherished children, her beloved husband, and her five cats. She finds precious time every day to escape into the medieval world and bring her characters to life in her writing.

She loves to hear from her readers! Find her on her website: **www.laurel-odonnell.com**, Facebook: **www.facebook.com/LaurelODonnell.author/** or Twitter: **twitter.com/laurelodonnell**

32171905R00111

Made in the USA
Middletown, DE
04 January 2019